To his surprise, ⸻
box-room, two p⸻
not recognise.

One was large, with a Coat-of-Arms in the center which someone had attempted to scrape away with a knife.

There was a sudden noise from inside the box which sounded like a sneeze.

The Viscount was startled.

Surprisingly easily, the top of the box came up in his hand.

A young woman was seated in the center of the box, surrounded by cushions.

She looked at him and said in an irritable voice:

"It is the feathers in these cushions. They keep on tickling my nose and I could not help sneezing!"

A Camfield Novel of Love by Barbara Cartland

———

"Barbara Cartland's novels are all distinguished by their intelligence, good sense, and good nature...."
— **ROMANTIC TIMES**

"Who could give better advice on how to keep your romance going strong than the world's most famous romance novelist, Barbara Cartland?"
— **THE STAR**

Camfield Place,
Hatfield
Hertfordshire,
England

Dearest Reader,

Camfield Novels of Love mark a very exciting era of my books with Jove. They have already published nearly two hundred of my titles since they became my first publisher in America, and now all my original paperback romances in the future will be published exclusively by them.

As you already know, Camfield Place in Hertfordshire is my home, which originally existed in 1275, but was rebuilt in 1867 by the grandfather of Beatrix Potter.

It was here in this lovely house, with the best view in the county, that she wrote *The Tale of Peter Rabbit*. Mr. McGregor's garden is exactly as she described it. The door in the wall that the fat little rabbit could not squeeze underneath and the goldfish pool where the white cat sat twitching its tail are still there.

I had Camfield Place blessed when I came here in 1950 and was so happy with my husband until he died, and now with my children and grandchildren, that I know the atmosphere is filled with love and we have all been very lucky.

It is easy here to write of love and I know you will enjoy the Camfield Novels of Love. Their plots are definitely exciting and the covers very romantic. They come to you, like all my books, with love.

Bless you,

CAMFIELD NOVELS OF LOVE
by Barbara Cartland

A NEW CAMFIELD NOVEL OF LOVE BY

Barbara Cartland

Running from Russia

J
JOVE BOOKS, NEW YORK

RUNNING FROM RUSSIA

A Jove Book / published by arrangement with
the author

PRINTING HISTORY
Jove edition / July 1995

ISBN: 0-515-11660-2

A JOVE BOOK®
Jove Books are published by The Berkley Publishing Group,
200 Madison Avenue, New York, New York 10016.
JOVE and the "J" design are trademarks
belonging to Jove Publications, Inc.

PRINTED IN THE UNITED STATES OF AMERICA

10 9 8 7 6 5 4 3 2 1

Author's Note

As I have explained in this novel, the Russian behaviour over the Fort of Pandjeh was disgraceful.

That the Tsar, Alexander III, had broken his promise to Great Britain was received with a mixture of fury and dismay.

The Fort was taken brutally by a trick on the part of the Russian General and created a situation which made it seem that war between the two great Powers was inevitable.

It was at the last moment, through the clever diplomacy of the Viceroy of India, the Marquis of Dufferin, that it was avoided.

However, the wholesale slaughter of the Afghans awakened the British Government under Mr. Gladstone to improve the defence of India, over which they had been very lethargic.

The terror in the Balkans created by the infiltration of Russians and the fear of the Third Section is not exaggerated.

At the time, it deeply concerned the countries I have mentioned and it was to continue during the whole reign of Alexander III.

chapter one

1885

THE Viscount Bredon walked down the platform with the Diplomats and Statesmen who had come to see him off. He stopped at the carriage behind the engine in which he knew he was travelling.

Being Russian, it was not so impressive as those the British had now produced in their own country and in India.

Nevertheless he knew that it was comfortable.

At least he would have a quiet journey across the long, open Plains to the Frontier.

He could have returned to England by sea, which he would have enjoyed after his arduous time in St. Petersburg.

Yet there were other countries Lord Granville had arranged for him to visit.

The Secretary of State for the Foreign Office would be waiting for a report on each one, especially with regard to their attitude towards Russia.

The Viscount had been sent to St. Petersburg because the British feared they were on the brink of War over the Russians' behaviour in the East.

Lord Granville had said to him:

"You had better go to see what you can do, Bredon.

But for God's sake, do not make it worse than it is already."

"I will do my best," the Viscount answered.

As assistant to the Secretary of State for the Foreign Office, he was very proud of his position and very keen to show his ability.

He had, at the age of twenty-seven, already made his mark in Diplomatic circles by the way he had handled a number of what were known as "tricky situations."

Russia was, however, different, and a growing menace, as the British had realised for some time.

Yet the Government had believed optimistically that things could not be as bad as they appeared.

In fact, they had not really anticipated that what was happening in the East would become so important.

That the Cossacks had been gobbling up the small independent States one after another did not seem of great importance to the Gentlemen in Whitehall.

But now, at this moment, Russia was pressing on Eastwards to Merv.

From there they would quite easily be able to march into Afghanistan and occupy Herat.

If that happened, the next step was quite obviously India.

It was then that the British woke up and the Viscount was sent off to St. Petersburg.

"You will find Tsar Alexander III a very strange man," Lord Granville had warned him.

The Viscount thought that was certainly the understatement of the year.

The thirty-six-year-old Alexander III was a giant of a man, extremely proud of his physical strength.

His favourite tricks were to tear a pack of cards in his hands, bend an iron poker over his knees, and crush a silver *ruble*.

The first act he performed, however, when he became Tsar was to tear up an unsigned Manifesto lying on his Father's desk.

The kind-hearted Alexander II had made a provision for a limited form of Representative Government at National level.

His son intended to have none of that nonsense!

He was determined to be different in every way from his Father, and he certainly succeeded.

Every drop of blood in his veins was German.

Yet the Englishmen visiting St. Petersburg always said that he had the stubborn, enigmatic look of a Russian peasant.

That was how he liked to think of himself.

He grew a beard, and wore the baggy trousers and the checked blouses of the *muzhik*s.

He opened his reign with the persecution of the Jews that was unequalled anywhere in the world.

The Viscount had not believed the stories of the cruelty afflicted on these miserable people until he had actually arrived in Russia.

Then he learnt that thousands of Jews had been murdered and their property confiscated.

He was actually brave enough to talk to the Tsar about it.

He then realised that Alexander firmly believed a gigantic plot was being organised by international Jewry to end the Monarchy in every country.

The Tsar was obviously a fanatic on the subject.

The Viscount had therefore tried to concentrate on the position in the East.

But he could not get the Tsar to say exactly what he intended.

However, the Viscount learnt something else in secret.

The Russian Foreign Minister, on the Tsar's instructions, was encouraging Revolutionaries to act as Agents in stirring up trouble for the established Regime in the Balkans.

Russian Embassy Officials paid crowds to start riots.

Russian Army Officers opened gymnasiums, where they drilled boys and girls in guerrilla warfare.

These and a thousand other strange things were happening near home, and far worse was occurring in the East.

The Viscount was thinking as he said "good-bye" to those who were seeing him off that the sooner he got back to England and sanity, the better.

The Russians, however, were all waiting to make their "good-bye speech."

When he reached the last man he moved up the steps to his compartment and shut the door.

The window was down.

As the train began to puff and blow its way out of the Station, there was a cheer from those who had bidden him "good-bye."

He waved his hand in reply.

It was then with a sense of relief that he sat down in what was not a particularly luxurious compartment.

At least he was alone.

There was a bedroom opening out of it and beyond that a Box-Room, where his luggage would have been stored.

He looked round appraisingly, knowing this was to be his home for the next few days.

It was well known that the trains crossing the endless flat Plains of Western Russia were invariably late.

Also they were inclined to break down or to run out of fuel.

Whatever happened, the Viscount thought, he would have time to plan exactly what he would say in his Report to those who were waiting for it in the War Office.

He wished only that he was going straight back to England.

As it was Spring, he would be able to watch his

race-horses and ride those which were waiting for him in his Stables.

As it was, he had a number of Officials to see in Hungary, Austria, Germany, and France.

The only thing that cheered him up was the knowledge that none of them could be so difficult as those he had just experienced in Russia.

He knew that he had not been exaggerating when he said: "We are on the very brink of War!"

The train was now increasing its speed.

The Viscount went into the small pantry which opened out of the Sitting-Compartment.

He found, as he expected, his Servant had left him a number of drinks, three bottles of Champagne, and one of Brandy.

The Russian trains were not as up-to-date as those on the Continent and in India.

There was no arrangement made for a Servant even for the most important travellers.

The Viscount's Valet had therefore to find accommodation in the next carriage rather than in the one which his Master was travelling.

It meant a lot of jumping in and out whenever the train stopped either at a Station or for fuel.

It was also inconvenient, as the Viscount felt now, when he had to open a bottle of Champagne himself.

It was not as cold as he liked, but he felt he needed some stimulation.

He had extracted himself with difficulty from the Russian Diplomats, who all told him a different story.

He could never be certain if he was hearing the truth.

He, in fact, suspected every confidence he was given.

He was convinced that he could not trust any Russian with whom he had discussed the possibility of War.

Having drunk a glass of Champagne, he corked up the bottle.

He went to where his bed was situated so that he could take off the formal coat he was wearing which proclaimed him as a Diplomat.

He had known only too well that he would be seen off by the Russians in all their glory.

They would have been very surprised if he had not been ornamented with gold braid and decorations.

His bed looked rather small and uncomfortable and he was quite sure the mattress would be hard.

But that was a minor discomfort.

He had learnt in his travels never to expect too much from any country except his own.

He took off his coat and threw it down on the bed.

Then he looked round to see if there was something lighter and more comfortable that he could put on.

To his annoyance, he found that his Servant had unpacked his Dressing-Case but none of his trunks.

His ivory-crested hair-brushes were laid out on the Dressing-Table; so were the shoe-horn and the button hook which matched them.

There was nothing in the cupboard in which his clothes should be hung.

He therefore opened the door into where the luggage had been put.

It was not a large space.

The Viscount travelled with clothes for every occasion, as he was never quite certain what he would be expected to do next.

He had known, however, that there would be good horses to ride in Russia.

His Riding-Boots had certainly taken up a great deal of room.

So had the Court Dress for different occasions, from the very important meeting with the Tsar to those with the Diplomats.

Although Alexander III wished to look like a peasant, he did not allow those in attendance on him to be anything but formal.

The Viscount had attended huge parties at the Winter Palace.

They were, he thought, as elaborate and colourful as they must have been in the reign of Catherine the Great.

Looking at his trunks, the Viscount wondered which one contained the comfortable, loose jacket he wore when he was alone or working at his desk.

To his surprise, he saw two pieces of luggage which he did not recognise.

One he was quite certain was not his.

It was large, almost square, and made of dark, nearly black, leather.

He was aware it was expensive, but he had never bought it himself.

Frowning, he thought that some fool had mixed some other person's luggage up with his.

This might cause an endless commotion if, as he suspected, the person in question was of any importance.

He looked to see if there was any label on the box.

He could not find one.

What he did see was that on the centre of it there had been a Coat-of-Arms which had been crudely scraped over with a knife.

The Viscount rubbed his fingers over the place.

Although he was certain it would originally have identified its owner, it had now been too mutilated to be of any help.

He had bent down to look at it.

Now, as he straightened himself, there was a sudden noise from inside the box which sounded like a sneeze.

The Viscount was startled.

Then he told himself he must have been mistaken.

It could only have been a noise outside the carriage which had seemed to him to have come from the inside.

To his astonishment, the sound came again.

Now he was convinced that it came from inside the box.

He saw it was closed in a strange manner and that where a key should have turned in the lock, there was no lock.

He bent forward and pulled at the top of the box.

It came up in his hand surprisingly easily.

As it did so, he was aware that looking up at him, there was a woman.

For a moment he was too astonished to say anything, but could only stand, staring at her.

She was seated in the centre of the box surrounded by cushions which enveloped her up to her shoulders.

She must, before he had opened the box, have had her head bent forward.

She looked at him and said in an irritable voice:

"It is the feathers in these cushions. They keep on tickling my nose and I could not help sneezing."

"Who are you? What are you doing here?" the Viscount asked.

To his surprise, the woman smiled at him and replied:

"I should have thought that was obvious! In case I start sneezing again, I think I had better get out of this extremely uncomfortable piece of luggage."

She rose up as she spoke.

Then, as the train was swaying a little, she put out her hand for the Viscount to help her.

Although he was bemused into silence, the Viscount did what was expected of him.

The young woman said:

"I think I am going to sneeze again. Actually I am dying of thirst. Please give me something to drink."

The door to the luggage room was open and she walked out along the passage.

The Viscount followed her, wondering what he should do.

In all his adventures, this was something which had never happened to him before.

As they reached the Sitting-Compartment, the young woman sneezed several times, putting a lace-edged handkerchief up to her nose as she did so.

The Viscount went to the cupboard in the pantry.

He opened the bottle of Champagne and poured out a glass. When he took it to her, she was no longer sneezing.

He realised for the first time that she was extremely pretty and also very young.

"Champagne!" she exclaimed when she saw what he was holding in his hand. "How delicious! It is something I really need. I should have known, as I have Hay-Fever, that I should not have used pillows with feathers in them."

"Now, what is all this about?" the Viscount said. "And what are you doing in the Luggage-Room of my carriage?"

"I am running away," she answered, "and I want you to take me back to England."

The Viscount stared at her.

"You must be aware," he replied, "that I can do nothing of the sort!"

"Why not?"

"Because I have been on a Diplomatic visit to St. Petersburg and I can hardly use my position to smuggle you out of the country, if that is what you want me to do."

"I thought you would be rather stuffy!" she said. "I was terrified you would find out I was there before the train left. But now, unless some of those abominable spies guess where I am, I am safe once we are out of Russia."

The Viscount put his fingers up to his forehead.

"It is not as easy as that," he said. "While I am extremely sorry for you, if there are reasons for you to wish to leave Russia, I cannot, in my position, do anything to help you."

"Rubbish," the woman said, "and apart from being stuck-up over your job, and all that nonsense, I think

9

as it is English blood calling to English blood, it would be a most un-gentlemanly act not to help me."

"What do you mean by 'English blood to English blood'?" the Viscount enquired.

"I am Princess Yentha Kerenska," the young woman replied. "My Father was a Cousin of the Tsar's, but my mother was English. In fact, she was the daughter of the Duke of Wilthorpe."

The Viscount realised he knew the present Duke slightly.

But he had registered the fact that she was a relative of the Tsar's.

That, he told himself, was what really mattered.

"Why are you running away?" he asked.

"I will tell you exactly," the Princess replied. "Then perhaps you will understand what a desperate situation I am in."

The Viscount thought that was no excuse to make it desperate for him too.

He did not say anything, and she went on:

"As you know, or should know by now, everywhere there are spies, and spies spying on spies! One of the spies who I believe is on my side informed me that the Tsar, who has never liked me, intended to give me as a wife to one of the Eastern Rulers with whom he is currying favour because, by doing so, he may help him succeed in conquering India."

The Viscount stared at her.

"You cannot be serious!"

"Of course I am serious," the Princess replied. "You cannot be so stupid as to not be aware that everything the Tsar said to you about his having no ambitions in the East is untrue."

"Again I cannot believe you because you are exaggerating," the Viscount said.

"In which case I will tell you something which I do not think you know, but which happens to be the truth," the Princess said, pausing before she continued:

10

"I am sure you were told by the Tsar and everyone else with whom you discussed it, that St. Petersburg has given a solemn assurance that their Armies would not attack Pandjeh provided the Afghans refrained from hostilities."

The Viscount nodded. This was certainly true.

He had had this repeated and repeated ever since he had arrived at the Winter Palace.

"I expect you also know," the Princess went on, "that Queen Victoria telegraphed to the Tsar appealing to him to prevent the calamity of a War."

The Viscount did not know this had happened, although the idea had been mooted before he had left England.

The Princess saw the answer in his eyes, and she said:

"Now I will tell you what I learnt had occurred yesterday and which you will not know for some time."

The Viscount waited apprehensively.

"There was only one way in which, having given their word to you and to so many other people, the Russians could justify an attack on Pandjeh. The Afghans had to be seen as the aggressors."

"What are you saying?" the Viscount asked. "It cannot be true that Pandjeh has fallen."

"It is in Russian hands," the Princess replied, "because, knowing the Afghans were both proud and quick-tempered, the Russian Commander wrote a highly offensive and insulting letter to their Commander and according to them, the Afghans opened fire, wounding the horse of one of the Cossacks."

The Viscount was listening apprehensively.

" 'Blood has been shed,' the Russian General declared," the Princess continued, "and gave orders for his Troops to open fire on the Afghan Cavalry. They broke and fled and the Russians gradually overran their positions."

"I cannot believe it," the Viscount murmured.

11

"Last night the Tsar was told secretly, and it is not yet to be announced," the Princess went on. "There were eight hundred dead, and many of them drowned while trying to escape across the flooded river. The Russian casualties amounted to only forty dead and wounded."

The Viscount was speechless.

He knew it would be weeks before this news reached London.

When it did, it would produce a situation of the utmost gravity.

"When I learnt this," the Princess was saying, "I knew that the moment had come when I had to escape or find myself married to some Ruler who would doubtless be the next to be butchered in the Russian Advance towards India."

"I find it difficult to believe that what you are telling me could be the truth," the Viscount said.

At the same time, he had the uncomfortable feeling that it was exactly how the Russians would behave.

In fact, he was a fool to be surprised at it.

Because he could think of nothing to say for the moment, he went back to the cupboard in the pantry.

He collected the bottle of Champagne and his own glass.

He then filled up the Princess's and, putting the bottle on the table between them, sat down next to her.

"I am sorry," she said, "if I have taken your breath away. But if you had lived in St. Petersburg for as long as I have, you would realise that they say one thing and do another. The Tsar in particular has an unquenchable ambition to conquer the whole world."

"I realised that myself," the Viscount said, "but I did not think he would go back on his word—not to take Pandjeh."

The Princess merely looked at him with a little twist to her lips.

He knew she was thinking that he was very naïve.

"I quite understand your predicament," the Viscount said, "but you must realise that although I am on my way back to England, I have a number of Diplomatic Contacts to make on the way. I cannot arrive with a run-away Princess! So perhaps the best thing you could do would be to get out of this carriage at the next stop."

The Princess threw back her head and laughed.

"Do you really think I would do anything so stupid? I have been seeking desperately for a way to escape for the last three weeks, ever since I knew what the Tsar had in mind. Now I have escaped with you and, as I cannot travel alone, you will just have to put up with me."

"Please be sensible," the Viscount replied.

He felt his temper rising.

At the same time, he knew as a Diplomat he had to play this accordingly.

"As I have just said," he went on, "I cannot arrive as a Representative of the Queen of England with a very young and beautiful woman. Your Highness must leave me. If it is a question of money, I will give you some."

"I have some money with me," the Princess said, "and my jewels, which are very valuable. But if I walk about alone with no-one to protect me, you know as well as I do, I shall be robbed and very likely killed."

She spoke in a quiet way which made it more impressive than if she had sounded terrified.

"Then what do you suggest I do?" the Viscount asked, speaking almost through gritted teeth.

"Perhaps the easiest way would be to say that we are married," the Princess replied.

The Viscount stared at her.

"Married!"

"Why not? There is no rule as far as I know about a Diplomat not having a wife."

The Viscount felt that his head was reeling.

He had long ago made up his mind, despite quite

a lot of pressure from his family, that he would not be married, not, at least, until his days of roaming all over the world on diplomatic Missions were finished.

What he was really thinking, although he did not put it into words, was, when his Father died, he would come into the ancient Earldom of Bredonhurst.

He would then have a huge Estate to administer.

He would also have to move into the House of Lords, where he could become a Senior Statesman.

He therefore confined his love affairs—and there had been a number of them—to the Beauties who circled round Marlborough House.

The Prince of Wales had made it possible for a Gentleman to have a love affair with a woman of his own Class.

The Viscount, who had always been very fastidious, found this was what he preferred.

He had always disliked what had been the fashion of having a Courtesan in a secret little house in St. John's Wood or Chelsea.

He also found the conversation of such women bored him to distraction.

He enjoyed the flirtatious wit of the Beauties who made the Prince of Wales laugh.

They had in his own experience the expertise which was rivalled only by the French.

Marriage was something he had put completely out of his mind.

Although his elder relations begged him incessantly to produce an heir, he told them there was plenty of time for that.

If he had fallen at the "roadside" on one of his more dangerous Missions, he had a younger brother who could very ably take his place.

Now this woman, who had thrust herself upon him, was suggesting of all things that she should pretend to be his wife.

Although it seemed absurd, he was almost shocked at the idea.

It was bad enough to think of the Russians lying to him with every word they spoke.

He had no wish to sink to their level.

Unless it was completely and absolutely necessary, he never lied in the service of his country.

He realised the Princess was waiting for him to speak, and he said:

"That is impossible! Your Highness must think of something else."

"You think of it," she answered. "As you say, we can hardly arrive to stay at an Embassy—if that is what you are doing—saying you have brought your Mistress with you! I see no reason why they should be shocked or startled if it was your wife."

"It would not be true," the Viscount said, "and of course, sooner or later they would realise that I had deceived them."

"There is no reason why they should probe into your private life afterwards," the Princess said. "I expect you will get married sooner or later. There is no reason, unless you are very stupid, why they should suspect we are not man and wife."

"It is a part I do not want to play," the Viscount said coldly. "So as I have already suggested, you must think of something else."

"That is for you to do," the Princess retorted. "I have put forward a very sensible proposition which will help me and, as I have already said, I am appealing to you as an English Gentleman. Is that not what all Englishmen want to be when they grow up?"

The Viscount realised that she was deliberately provocative.

He arose from where he was sitting.

He walked across the carriage to the further window.

They were already out in the wilds, and there was no sign of any human habitation.

He suddenly thought that when the Tsar had discovered that the Princess was missing, one of the

Spies might suggest she was with him.

In which case the Russian Secret Police would be following them.

He turned round.

As if the Princess could read his thoughts, she said:

"The Tsar will not discover until tomorrow morning that I am not in the Palace."

"How can you be sure of that?" the Viscount asked.

"My maid, whom I can trust because she has been with me since I was a child, has told the Servants in the Palace that I have a bad attack of Hay-Fever. She has therefore put me to bed and given me a sleeping draught which ensures that I will sleep peacefully until tomorrow."

The Viscount had to concede it had at least made things a little better than they might be.

At the same time, they would not be out of Russia for at least three days.

If the Tsar telegraphed down the line, which he could do to some stations, the Police would be waiting for them on the platform.

The Princess knew what was troubling the Viscount.

"I can cross to London in the box in which you found me," she said. "I need become your wife only when we are no longer on Russian soil."

"I will not have you travelling with me," the Viscount said.

Then, as he spoke, he knew he was losing the battle.

"We have a long time to think about it," the Princess said, "and I presume like most Englishmen you can trust your Servant."

"He is the only person I do trust at the moment," the Viscount said bitterly. "At the same time, he should not have allowed your luggage to be placed with mine."

"It was done very skilfully, under my instructions," the Princess answered. "My maid, whom I have just told you I can trust, came into the Station and asked him to inspect a piece of luggage which she thought had your name on it at the other end of the platform."

She paused before she went on:

"While he was doing this, they were putting the rest of your luggage in place. The two men who drove the cart were extremely stupid and put me down rather roughly, I thought, in the Luggage-Room."

The Viscount had to admit to himself that she had at least thought of every detail.

In fact, he thought it very unusual for a woman to be so intelligent.

After all, it was a very difficult and complicated method of escape.

He supposed, being desperate, she had chosen the only chance she had of getting away from St. Petersburg.

The Tsar's plan for her marriage to help him in his subjection of the countries between Russia and India was disgraceful.

It was, however, as the Viscount knew, genuine.

He still found it very hard to believe, after all that had been said, that the Russians had dared to seize Pandjeh.

In India he was aware that two Army Corps, one under General Roberts, had been mobilised in readiness to march across Afghanistan to defend Herat if it was necessary.

He could only think now that the necessity was there.

Perhaps too late the British were aware that they should have strengthened the defence of Pandjeh. The Princess was watching his face.

"Mama always said," she remarked, "that the British were far too trusting and were inclined to do what was right rather than what was expedient. The Russians have caught you napping and I am wondering what you can do about it."

The Viscount knew the answer.

17

He could only pray that it would not be an Anglo-Russian War.

"I know what you are thinking," the Princess said, "and I am very sympathetic. At the same time, I might be able to help you."

"After all, I am half Russian. I know their treacherous, tricky ways, especially when they are ruled by someone like the present Tsar."

The Viscount thought it was very unlikely that she could help him in any way at all.

At the same time, she was making a pleasant gesture.

He could not be bad mannered enough not to be polite to her.

"Thank you," he said, "I will accept gratefully any help you can give me, and, of course, I will do my best to help you."

"And that is quite easy," the Princess said almost triumphantly. "You just accept me as your wife before we reach England."

The Viscount thought they should be stopping in a short time. His Servant would then come and prepare dinner for him.

It had been brought to the train packed in hay-baskets and was waiting for Bates to unpack it.

He would serve it to his Master with the same elegance he would have done at home.

The Viscount pulled his watch out of his waistcoat pocket.

He was aware for the first time since he had found the Princess that he was in a state of undress.

"I think," he said, "we should be stopping in the next ten minutes or quarter of an hour. I want my Servant to unpack some clothes I require, in the Luggage-Room. So I imagine it would be best if you went back to where I found you."

"As I intend to eat my dinner with you," the Princess answered, "I see no reason, if you can trust your

18

Servant as you say you can, why he should not meet me now?"

The Viscount did not reply, and she went on:

"He will meet me when we arrive, and it is essential he should help us if the Secret Police come aboard, as you think they might, before we have left Russia."

"What do you intend to do then?" the Viscount asked with an edge in his voice.

"I shall, of course, hide in the box in which you found me, but it will be very uncomfortable if your man was asked what was in it and he said he did not know, and that he had no idea why it came aboard."

The Viscount had to admit this was common-sense.

At the same time, he told himself that he should be thinking of these details and not a woman.

He looked at her and realised by the twinkle in her eyes that she was amused at what he was feeling.

"You have got me into an incredible mess," he said angrily.

"I am sorry! I am so sorry!" the Princess cried. "It would have been far worse for me to be pushed off on some drug-taking, dark-skinned Emir who would doubtless have a Harem of other women and take the first opportunity he could of executing me."

"I cannot believe it would be as bad as that," the Viscount said.

"I have every reason to think it might be worse," the Princess said, "and therefore, as I have to fight for myself, I will fight with every weapon in my power, and, of course, if necessary, this!"

She pulled, as she spoke, a small pistol out of the pocket of her gown.

It was very small and covered with jewels.

The Viscount recognised it as one of the special pistols that were made in Russia with great skill for the Imperial Family.

"Do you know how to use it?" he asked.

"Very well indeed," the Princess replied. "You forget I am half English, and my Mother often told me

19

what extremely good game-shots all her family were."

"Why on earth did your Mother marry a Russian?" the Viscount enquired.

It sounded rather a rude question, but the Princess smiled.

"My Father came to England at the invitation of Queen Victoria. He happened to be in Buckingham Palace when my Mother was presented at Court. He fell in love at first sight, and so did my Mother. They were extremely happy, and although there was a great deal about Russia that my Mother disliked, she was completely content to be with my Father."

"Then what happened?" the Viscount enquired.

"My Father was killed in some hare-brained, idiotic ride the Cossacks took in bad weather over the swollen rivers and up the sides of icy mountains. It was a challenge he had to accept because he was such an outstanding rider. When he was . . . killed his . . . death . . . destroyed . . . my Mother."

Her voice was very moving as she said quietly:

"She loved . . . him . . . so much. She could . . . not go on . . . living in . . . this world . . . without him."

"I am sorry!" the Viscount said.

"I was left to be brought up in the Winter Palace, and last year, when I had finished my schooling, I was aware that the Tsar was looking at me and wondering how I would come in useful."

There was silence.

Looking at her, the Viscount realised she was a very strange mixture of English and Russian.

Her hair was dark, very soft and silky with mauve lights in it.

Her eyes, fringed with dark lashes, were a deep blue, and must have been inherited from her Mother.

Her skin was pearly white and a vivid contrast to the darkness of her hair.

Because she was speaking of her Father and Mother, her voice had softened and so had her face.

The Viscount thought it would be difficult to find any woman, anywhere, who was quite so lovely.

At the moment, because she was thinking of those who had left her, she had a spiritual look which he had seldom seen before.

In England she would be a huge success, he told himself.

He was aware that she would certainly join and eclipse what were called the "Professional Beauties." They had attracted so much public attention that people stood on chairs in the Park to see them drive past.

Then he told himself that he was being weak in accepting that he should take her to England.

It was something he could not do.

"I must think of some other way she can reach there without me," he told himself. "It should not be difficult."

He knew, however, as he went on looking at her, that it would be quite impossible for her to travel without the protection of a man.

That did not mean a Servant.

"I cannot do it! It is impossible!" he said silently.

He knew the words were hollow.

Vaguely he thought that perhaps the best thing would be to take her straight to England and deposit her with her relations.

He could then return to his duty in the other parts of Europe.

Then he remembered what she had just told him.

Because the Russians had tricked everybody and seized Pandjeh, the whole situation had changed.

He had to be in touch with the other countries allotted to him by Lord Granville as swiftly as possible.

He knew he was right in thinking that it would be a week or perhaps longer before London was aware of what had happened.

He could imagine the fury and dismay with which the news would be received.

The person who would be most angry of all would be Her Majesty the Queen.

"What can I do? What the Devil can I do?"

He said the words to himself, but the Princess stretched out her hand.

"I am sorry to worry you," she said. "But please believe me when I tell you everything will come all right in the end."

The Viscount thought that this was very unlikely.

The Princess's blue eyes were beseeching him, and her hand was on his.

"We can only hope for the best," he replied.

He felt, as he spoke, that he had not been very generous.

In fact, he had the uneasy feeling that he was not behaving like a Gentleman.

The train came slowly to a halt.

Bates climbed up into the carriage.

When he saw the Princess, his jaw dropped.

He was a small, wiry little man who had been with the Viscount ever since he had left Oxford.

He was always good tempered, never at a loss.

As the Viscount knew, he could be relied on completely and trusted as he could trust no-one else.

"I want your help, Bates," he said before the Valet could speak.

"This is Her Highness Princess Yentha Kerenska, who has run away from St. Petersburg and has to reach her relations in England. When it is discovered she is missing, we may be followed by the Secret Police."

"That'd not surprise me, M'Lord," Bates said. "They be like crawling lizards wherever yer look, and I wouldn't trust one of 'em in th' dark."

"That is what the Princess is feeling now," the Viscount said, "and before you ask the question, she came here in a box that was put in with mine while her maid was showing you some luggage at the other end of the platform."

"Tricks! Always tricks!" Bates exclaimed. "If one don't work, they tries another."

"Now, what we have been thinking," the Viscount went on as if he had not spoken, "is that Her Highness must, of course, hide in the trunk where I found her. But when we leave Russia we have to find an explanation of why she is travelling with me."

As he spoke, the Viscount could not help hoping optimistically that Bates would not fail him.

He would find some magical explanation which had not occurred to him.

"That's certainly a hard one, M'Lord," Bates said reflectively.

He was looking at the Princess as he spoke.

Once again the Viscount, irritated as he was by her presence, could not help but admit that she was beautiful.

"Well, M'Lord, 'tis like this," Bates said at length, "you can hardly pass Her Highness off as one of yer children, so it has to be as yer wife."

The Princess gave a cry of delight and clapped her hands.

"Well done!" she exclaimed. "That is exactly what I have been saying to His Lordship, and he would not believe me."

"I can't think of anythin' else," Bates said, "and there be no law, as far as I knows, that a Diplomat can't take 'is wife with 'im on a long journey."

"No, of course not," the Princess agreed. "It will be quite easy, as you will see. I will behave exactly as if I were a well-brought up, rather dull Englishwoman, and there is no reason for anyone to suspect that I am half Russian."

"There ain't many English women as looks like you, Your Highness," Bates said. "They'd give their eyeteeth to do so if they could."

The Princess bowed her head.

"Thank you, Bates. That is a very pretty compliment, and the first one I have received since I boarded this train.''

She glanced over her eye-lashes at the Viscount as she spoke.

He said almost sharply:

''This may sound a joke, but actually it is very serious! I know Your Highness will not mind me telling Bates that the Russians have taken Pandjeh after their promises that it was something they would not do.''

''That does not surprise me, M'Lord,'' Bates said. ''The last words everyone says to me before I left England was 'yer can't trust a Russian.' I haven't met one yet as didn't lie like a trooper.''

The Princess laughed, and the Viscount could not help smiling.

Bates always mixed up his metaphors.

Yet there was no doubt that he hit the nail on the head every time.

The Viscount pulled out his watch from his waist-coat pocket.

''Unless I am wrong,'' he said, ''we should be arriving at the first stop in two or three minutes time.''

He looked at the Princess and said:

''In case there are Secret Police who ask questions, I think you should hide yourself.''

As he spoke, he thought for the first time that he was taking command.

It was a good thing that he did.

The Princess gave a little cry.

Jumping up, she put her empty glass into Bates's hand and ran towards the Luggage-Room.

By the time the Viscount joined her, she was already back in the box with the cushions round her.

She looked up at him, waiting for him to close the top of the box over her head.

Even as he put out his hand he felt the train begin to slow down.

''I do not think we shall stay here long,'' he said.

"If you hear somebody moving about, be careful not to sneeze."

"I will be very careful," she said. "I can assure you the Police will not be as polite as you."

She was smiling as she spoke.

The Viscount knew she was appreciating the fact that she had won the battle and he had surrendered.

He was taking the responsibility for her.

If they were fortunate enough to escape from Russia, he would have to do what she asked and accept her as his wife.

The train was coming slowly to a standstill.

He began to tip the top of the box forward.

As he did so, he said a little wryly:

"I had no choice, did I?"

"None!" she answered.

He shut the lid on her.

chapter two

THE train came to a standstill.

Looking out of the window, the Viscount saw two people on the platform climb into a Lower-class carriage.

There appeared to be only two men who might be Porters at the end of the train, and no-one came near him.

As the train started to move on again, Bates said:

"Well, M'Lord, that's that! And no hard feelings."

"We still have to be very careful, Bates," the Viscount replied.

Bates nodded and said:

"Yer can't be too careful with them there Ruskies. I wouldn't trust 'em an inch."

It was only as the train was some way on that the Viscount realised that Bates had stayed in his carriage and not gone to his own.

He imagined it was because he had to clean up the plates and glasses from Luncheon.

Then, as he was thinking that now the Princess would appear, Bates said:

"I thinks, M'Lord, it'd be a good idea, if them Russian Police be after yer, Oi made meself a place to lie down with the luggage."

The Viscount looked at him in surprise.

Then he realised he was talking sense.

If the Secret Police were waiting for them anywhere, he would certainly need Bates to support him.

At the same time, he was well aware that if they got into the clutches of the Russian Police, there would be no hope of doing anything but surrender.

One of the things the Viscount had done very carefully before he became involved in any way with Russian Diplomacy was to learn of their system of Spying.

It was more frightening than anything else anywhere in the world.

Nicholas I, who had become Tsar in 1825, had been a despot and a tyrant.

He was an extremely cruel and unpleasant man, but he did not depend wholly on his own powers of observation.

He streamlined the Secret Police and formed a new department known as the Third Section.

He had a friend who was as tyrannical as he was, and he put him in charge.

He told him to act as the "Nation's Moral Physician" in every town in Russia.

At the time the Death Penalty had not been revived, but it was well-known that a man could be killed by the *knout*.

The Third Section took it upon itself to censor everything either written or spoken which they considered critical of the Government and the Tsar.

They had Spies in every possible place.

Men could be arrested on the merest whisper if it was thought to be subversive.

The Third Section had lapsed a little under Alexander II.

It had come back with Alexander III, and now was a menace that lurked behind every door. No man was safe from it.

The Viscount was thinking of this when the Princess came into the compartment.

"I did not sneeze," she said, "although I gather there was no-one to hear me if I had."

"You were lucky," the Viscount replied, "but that is no reason not to take precautions."

"No, of course not!" the Princess agreed.

"I was just wondering," the Viscount said rather casually. "Do you really think when the Tsar discovers that you are missing, he will send the Police to look for you?"

"You can be quite certain he will do that," the Princess replied. "If there is one thing that infuriates him, it is if he does not get his own way in every small particular."

The Viscount was silent, and she said:

"I know exactly what you are thinking! Unfortunately he will definitely send the Third Section after me."

"What will they do when they find you?" the Viscount enquired.

"They will either take me back and make me marry the Eastern Potentate the Tsar has chosen for me, or else I shall just disappear."

"You mean they will kill you?" the Viscount enquired.

The Princess nodded.

The Viscount sat down in one of the armchairs.

"Now, listen," he said. "Are you not making a mistake to risk your life in this way?"

"I have to escape! I have to!" the Princess replied.

She slipped into the chair next to his and clasped her hands together.

"Can you imagine what it would be like being taken off to some ghastly Eastern man who very probably cannot speak my language any more than I can speak his?"

The Viscount did not answer, and after a moment she went on:

"If I have to die—and if I am dragged back to St. Petersburg—it may be by my own hand. I would rather die cleanly from a bullet, although I doubt if the Third Section will ask which I prefer."

"I find it hard to believe all this," the Viscount said.

He was wondering frantically if he ought to speak about her in person to the Tsar.

It would be possible in any civilised country.

He was, however, quite certain Alexander III would not listen.

The stories about him, despite the danger of repeating them, had been poured into his ears from the moment he had arrived in St. Petersburg.

A great number had seemed at first to be quite amusing.

He was told that the Tsar was frugal to the point of miserliness.

He had issued orders that soap and candles must be used up before they were thrown away, and table linen was not to be changed every day.

The lights were not to be left burning in empty rooms.

There was no small detail that did not come under his scrutiny.

He ordered that twenty people did not require an omelette made with as many as one hundred eggs.

There was always someone at his table who got very little to eat.

Apart from this, his guests frequently complained that the food was inedible.

The Viscount had been particularly touched by a story about the Tsar's son and heir, Nicholas, who was thirteen.

He was so hungry that he opened the Gold Cross given to him at his Baptism and ate the Beeswax inside.

His sister, the Grand Duchess Olga, explained that it was an Act of Blasphemy. A tiny relic of the True Cross was embedded in the wax.

She made Nicholas feel ashamed of himself, but he also said that it tasted "immortally good."

There were so many stories about the Tsar that the Viscount had ceased to listen to them.

He thought they were just Russian imagination.

He was to learn more about the horrors that were taking place in St. Petersburg in the next few days.

He also learnt a great deal about Russian Army movements which he knew would be of interest to Lord Granville when he reached England.

The Princess was only too willing to talk about her life in the Palace since her Father and Mother died.

She knew secrets which European Diplomats would have given their ears to hear.

Like all tyrants, Alexander III was devoted to his wife and five children; he had had six, but one died in 1871.

When he was with them he relaxed completely, talking apparently in what the Viscount thought was an extremely indiscreet manner.

He had discovered for himself that the Empress was very badly educated.

She therefore seldom thought for herself but merely echoed her husband's prejudices.

The Viscount could understand that, as the Princess was so young and was virtually one of the family, it never occurred to the Tsar for one moment to guard his tongue when she was present.

As she chattered on, and she was, he had to admit, extremely interesting, the Viscount felt slightly guilty at what he was hearing.

At the same time, he had little choice but to listen.

There had been a crisis the first evening when daylight began to fade.

It was not until then that the Viscount, bemused by what was happening, realised there was only one bed.

As he looked at it again, he supposed the Russians had thought it could be occupied by two people who were travelling together.

But in his case he had to give it up to the Princess.

31

When he told her that was what he intended to do, she protested.

"No, of course not!" she said. "I imposed myself on you, and I am quite prepared to sleep on the floor. I have, as you well know, lots of feather pillows with me."

"Which will make you sneeze all night!" the Viscount said. "That will undoubtedly keep me awake!"

"I cannot be so selfish as to take your bed," the Princess said.

It was, of course, Bates who solved the problem.

A sofa was at the back of the wall in the Sitting-Compartment.

Bates discovered that the sides could be let down, which made it into a bed when required.

"That is clever of you, Bates," the Viscount exclaimed. "I never thought of that. As it is, the sofa would be very uncomfortable for my long legs."

"Yer'll be comfortable, all right, M'Lord," Bates said. "One thing, as it's warm at this time o' the year, they provides plenty of blankets for when the place is thick with snow."

The sofa was, the Viscount had to admit, quite as comfortable, if not better, than the bed.

The Princess had a room to herself.

Therefore, the fact that they were together unchaperoned was less obvious than it might have been.

At the same time, when the Viscount had been with her for two days, he realised how very young and innocent she was.

She was also completely unselfconscious.

It amused him to realise that while she had plenty to say, she did not treat him as an attractive man with whom she should flirt.

The Viscount had these last years been continually with beautiful, attractive, and sophisticated women, not only in England, but in Paris, Rome, Vienna, and a great number of other cities.

He was used to the *double entendre*.

Every conversation would invariably concern love.

He would have been extremely stupid, which he was not, if he had not realised that he was outstandingly handsome.

He was also naturally charming and good-mannered.

He was used to the glint in a woman's eye when she looked at him, the provocative little twist of her red lips, and the certain note in her voice which was an invitation in itself!

But with the Princess it was quite different.

She talked to him eagerly and listened attentively.

She never attempted in any way to draw attention to herself as a woman.

He did not think that it had ever occurred to her that he was an attractive man.

She was using him to escape from what he realised was an intolerable situation.

She was grateful.

At the same time, he felt she would have behaved exactly the same if she had been with her brother or her Father.

He thought wryly that it was good for his ego to be aware that she was not in any way trying to attract him.

'I must be getting old!' the Viscount thought with a smile.

The train steamed on through the night.

The next day it stopped only for fuel at some isolated place from which there could be seen the flat, dull Plains disappearing in a misty horizon and nothing more.

It was when they were near the Hungarian border that the Viscount began to be worried.

The Tsar by this time might suspect that the Princess had left the Palace with him.

If so, members of the Third Section would be waiting to examine him when he arrived at the Frontier.

Bates was clearing away supper.

It had not been particularly edible, as the food had now been kept for three days.

The Princess was finishing the last glass of Champagne.

The Viscount got up from the table and moved to the window.

"I have been reckoning," he said, "that we will soon be running short of fuel. We still have several hours to go before we reach Bistritz."

Both the Princess and Bates were listening.

"Therefore," he went on, "we have to decide how Your Highness can be hidden if the Spies who may be waiting for us inspect this compartment."

"Are you suggesting," the Princess asked in a rather frightened voice, "that I move into . . . another part . . . of the . . . train?"

"I was trying to think of how to prevent you being caught and taken back to St. Petersburg," the Viscount replied.

She gave a little cry.

"There must be something! I have been thinking too, and I am frightened. Very frightened! Oh, please! There must be . . . somewhere I can . . . hide!"

Bates, who had been listening as he took off the table-cloth, said:

"I have an idea, Your Highness, though yer may not like it."

"What is it?" the Viscount enquired.

He had been with Bates in many difficult situations. He had never known the little man not to come up with some idea, even if it was too complicated for use.

Bates leant against the table as if for support.

"Now, I were just thinking," he said, "that when them Ruskies comes to look for yer, they'll be looking for a pretty young woman."

"Are you suggesting," the Princess said, "that I disguise myself as a man?"

"It is an idea," the Viscount exclaimed, "but to begin with, my clothes would be much too big for you,

34

and secondly, whatever Bates may think, no-one would, for a moment, believe you to be of the masculine gender."

"Wait a second, M'Lord," Bates said, "I were not thinkin' of Her Highness being a man, but an old woman."

Both the Viscount and the Princess stared at him.

"How can you do that?" the Viscount asked.

"It rather depends on what Her Highness has in her trunk," Bates replied. "But I'm hoping that her has a veil. All the older women nowadays wears a veil."

That the Viscount knew was true.

It was the fashion when he had last been in London.

He had noticed that the Beauties with whom he drove in the Park, or lunched with in the smartest houses, wore veils over their faces.

It gave them, he thought, an alluring look they had not had before.

He had learnt that it was only a married woman who could wear a veil, just as she could wear a tiara and earrings which were forbidden to *débutantes* or those unfortunates who had not been able to catch themselves husbands.

Now, when he thought over what Bates had said, he exclaimed:

"You are a genius, Bates! I am sure you have your make-up box with you!"

"I have, M'Lord," Bates answered. "After all, us never knows when it might be wanted."

On various occasions on his travels the Viscount had wanted to be disguised, but not because he was being pursued by Russian Spies.

He had, however, wanted to visit some places where, as a Diplomat and an Englishman, he should not be seen.

Because he thought this was part of his education, he had gone disguised.

Sometimes it was as a man from a country whose language he could speak quite fluently.

He once went in fancy dress, which had undoubtedly been a great success.

"If the Princess'll come along with me now," Bates was saying, "I'll have a look in her trunk and see what us can find."

The Viscount did not offer to go with them.

He settled himself comfortably in a chair and thought how useful it was to have Bates with him.

He had certainly been extremely grateful to him for providing him with a bed.

Bates had assured him that he had been very comfortable in the Trunk-Room, as long as he could leave the door open to get some air.

The Viscount knew that, on the Princess's suggestion, he had slept on the cushions she had used in her large, box-like trunk.

When he thought about it, he was not certain that Bates had not got the best end of the deal.

He was certain now that Bates would be able to make the Princess look like an old lady.

Once they were over the Border and safely in Hungary, they should be able to evade any further investigations by the Russian Police.

Yet he was not sure this was possible.

He had been told in St. Petersburg that the Third Section never gave up.

They boasted that however long it took, they always eventually "got their man."

In this case, the Viscount told himself, they would have to be disappointed.

At the same time, he was worried and he knew that he certainly would not sleep that night.

It was an hour before the Princess came back to where he was sitting.

"Bates has arranged everything," she said. "I am to get out quickly at the last halt before we reach Bistritz and move into a Second-Class carriage which he says are not very full. It is doubtful if anyone will notice me."

Looking at her, the Viscount thought this was wish-ful thinking.

There was no doubt that with her blue eyes and her dark hair, she looked exceedingly pretty.

She had also, he discovered, two dimples on either side of her mouth when she laughed.

Her eyes seemed, with their dark lashes, almost too big for her small, pointed face.

"I suppose there is nothing else we can do," he said almost harshly.

"I cannot have come all this way to go back igno-miniously. The Tsar will be furious with me, and when he is furious, anything might happen."

There was a touch of terror in the Princess's voice which made the Viscount say soothingly:

"You will just have to trust Bates. He is brilliant at this sort of thing, and when he has disguised me, no-one has ever thought I was a tall, handsome Aristo-crat from England."

He was speaking mockingly to make her laugh.

She gave just a little chuckle before she said:

"Of course you had to disguise that you were a Gentleman!"

"Of course," the Viscount said, "I had forgotten that. I suppose I am not behaving like a Gentleman should at this moment. Otherwise I should imperson-ate you, allow myself to be arrested while you es-caped, telling everyone that you were the Viscount Bredon!"

The Princess laughed as he meant her to do, and some of the fear left her eyes.

The Viscount looked at her, and then he said:

"If the worse comes to the worst and you are taken back to St. Petersburg, I suggest you seek Sanctuary in the British Embassy. Ask them to be brave enough to tell the Tsar they must look after you."

"I had already thought of doing that after Mama died," the Princess said. "I wanted then to go to Eng-land, and when I suggested it in a roundabout way, the British Ambassador was not at all encouraging."

The Viscount's lips tightened.

He knew that as things were difficult at that moment between Britain and Russia, the Ambassador had no wish to make things worse than they were already.

The feelings of a young girl were of no particular importance.

They were certainly not to be considered when the question was whether there would be an Anglo-Russian War or not.

The Viscount must have been looking worried, because the Princess put her hand on his arm.

"I am sure," she said in a soft voice, "Papa and Mama helped me to find you. Wherever they are—and I do not think they are far away—they will be helping us . . . now."

"I hope you are right," the Viscount said.

"I shall pray very, very hard for myself," the Princess said, "and also that you will not get into any trouble with the Tsar because of me."

"Thank you," the Viscount said.

He was about to say something more, when Bates came up to him.

"I've got it all fixed, M'Lord," he said. "We must be ready at the place you thinks we'll stop at for Her Highness to leave."

"Yes, of course, Bates," the Viscount said. "I will leave it all to you. So far you have never failed!"

"Touch wood an' cross yer fingers," Bates said. "We can't let them there Spies beat us! Can we?"

"No, of course not!" the Viscount agreed.

They had their dinner which, as the Princess said, would be the last meal they would have together in the train.

"I have somehow got fond of this funny little place," she said. "It has been fun being with you, and if I am told I have to go back with two or three of the

Third Section, I think I shall throw myself under the engine."

"You are not to talk like that," the Viscount said sharply. "I have always been told that when you disguise yourself, your thoughts have to be as disguised as your appearance."

He paused for a moment and then continued:

"You will, therefore, from the moment that Bates helps you dress, be thinking the thoughts of an older woman. Otherwise those who are particularly perceptive may know that you are deceiving them."

"I understand what you are saying," the Princess said. "Of course you are right. I will think of myself as tired and elderly and how much better the old days were than these."

She smiled before she said provocatively:

"I shall think, of course, that young people like you are behaving very badly and not in the least as attentive as they were in my day."

The Viscount laughed.

"That is it exactly! When we get past the barrier, then we can find some way in which we can introduce ourselves to each other so that you will travel with me in the carriage which I suspect will be waiting from the Embassy."

"How shall I change to look as your wife should?" the Princess asked. "I can hardly keep up the pretence of being your Mother!"

"I will think of a way," the Viscount replied. "There will be a Hotel of some sort in Bistritz and we will go there first."

"I must tell Bates that is your idea," the Princess said.

They then went to bed.

The Viscount found himself tossing and turning on the sofa, finding it impossible to sleep.

He knew better than anyone else that they were courting danger.

To oppose the Tsar in his own country was the

equivalent of committing suicide.

It would be assumed, of course, that he had run away with the Princess because they were in love.

Nothing he or she could say could prevent the outside world knowing about it.

They would be told he had deliberately seduced one of the Tsar's relations and persuaded her to elope with him.

It would not only be the end of his career, the Viscount thought, it would also do immeasurable harm to the Diplomatic negotiations being carried on at the moment.

If he was to believe the Princess, Pandjeh had already fallen to the Russians.

There was every chance that War had broken out already between Russia and Britain.

He was hoping that the Diplomats who were entertaining him would know more of what had occurred in the East.

He had, however, the uneasy feeling that they would be in ignorance.

He was, too, staying privately, as there was no British Embassy in Bistritz.

He wished now that he had made more fuss about where he was going when he reached Hungary.

It had all been arranged for him in rather a hurry, and he had just accepted what was handed to him.

They knew he was arriving and would therefore be meeting him.

Somehow, in some clever way of which no-one would be suspicious, he had to produce a wife.

She had not been on the original itinerary.

"How on earth did I get myself into this mess!" the Viscount asked as he tossed and turned again.

He knew the answer.

He had behaved "like a Gentleman" in saving a damsel in distress.

It was still not dawn when he heard voices coming

from the Princess's Compartment, and he knew that Bates was with her.

Time ticked by as he got up to dress.

He began to think that perhaps he had made a mistake.

The train would not need refuelling and would carry straight on to Bistritz.

The sun was rising over the horizon when finally the door opened and Bates put his head round.

"Are you awake, M'Lord?" he enquired.

It was an unnecessary question, as the Viscount was standing by the window fully dressed.

He did not reply, and Bates opened the door wider.

"Here her is," he said. "Be careful of her, as she be getting on for sixty!"

The Princess came in.

One glance told the Viscount that Bates had once again excelled himself in the art of disguise.

Facing him was an old lady with white hair which only just showed beneath her hat, from the crown of which was a spotted veil covering her face.

The Viscount knew how skilful Bates was with his paints and pencils.

Otherwise he would not have doubted for a moment that the dark lines under the old lady's eyes, and the deep lines running from the nose to the chin, were completely genuine.

She was dressed in a dark cape and there was a black scarf round her neck.

It was the elegant veil which was the most disguising of all.

Bates had been clever enough to see that she was wearing gloves so that one could not see her young, unlined hands.

He had also produced an umbrella on which the elderly lady was leaning.

When the Princess saw the Viscount's face, she said:

"Tell me the truth! Would you have known it was me?"

"Of course I would not," the Viscount replied. "Well done, Bates! Now you will have to get her into another compartment."

He saw a little expression of anxiety in the Princess's eyes, and said:

"I am sure you will be all right. You know I cannot come with you."

"I shall be perfectly all right," the Princess answered. "It is just that I do not want you to drive away without me when we have passed through the Customs, as I expect that is where the Spies will be waiting."

The Viscount thought this was very likely.

"What I've been a thinkin', M'Lord," Bates said, "is it'd be best for Her Highness to go first, and for yer to saunter off, ever so casual-like, as if yer were in no hurry."

"That is a good idea!" the Viscount agreed. "The Spies, if they are there, will be waiting to see who I have with me. They will not concern themselves with the other travellers."

"That's exactly wot I thinks!" Bates agreed.

The train was beginning to slow down.

Bates disappeared to the bedroom to pick up a small case which he had packed for the elderly lady to carry.

It had to be light.

At the same time, she could have hardly gone on such a long journey without any clothes.

The Princess went nearer to the Viscount.

"I have been praying," she said, "but in case anything happens, thank you for being so kind. I have loved being in this funny little train with you and, of course, Bates."

The Viscount registered with a slight smile that most women would not have added Bates to their gratitude.

42

"He has been wonderful," the Princess went on. "He has made me feel quite sure we shall win this battle. It is actually the most important one."

She thought the Viscount would understand, but added:

"Of course I am still on . . . Russian . . . soil!"

"I am aware of that," he said. "Now, be ready to get down quickly. You know it would be a mistake for me to come on the platform to see you off."

"Yes, of course," the Princess agreed. "Keep out of sight, but please think about me."

"You can be sure I will do that," the Viscount replied.

The train got slower and slower, and he knew the Princess was looking agitated.

"I am sure there will be practically no-one on the platform," he said. "Any Official who is there ordinarily will be watching the fuel going on board."

The train came to a stop.

The doors of the carriages began to open.

Even if people were not stopping, most of them wished to stretch their legs.

Quite a number came to look at the huge logs being put aboard as fuel.

It was then the Princess slipped down the steps with an ease which would have been impossible for anyone of her assumed age.

The moment she was on the platform she moved very slowly, supported by her umbrella.

When he thought that no-one would be noticing him, the Viscount leant out of the window.

He looked first towards the engine puffing smoke into the air, and then quite casually down the length of the train.

A few carriages away he saw the Princess climbing up the steps, and as she reached the open door a kindly hand came out as if to assist her.

She was moving very cleverly, the Viscount thought, as if it were difficult for her to do so.

Then he told himself it would be a great mistake if anyone saw her looking in his direction.

He went inside his own carriage.

It was nearly three hours before they reached Bistritz.

To the Viscount it felt as if he had travelled a million miles in that time, and he had never known a clock to move so slowly.

Bates had packed up everything they had with them.

Then he had come to the Viscount, saying:

"I thinks, M'Lord, it'd be a mistake, if the Ruskies were about, for them to see this case. It'd not be what a Gentleman'd use. Looks to me, any Spy who had his 'ead on his shoulders would know it contained someone."

"You are quite right, Bates," the Viscount said. "Throw it out."

"That's exactly what I thinks yer Lordship'd say."

They were passing through what seemed a particularly rough piece of land, and there was still no sign of any habitation.

Bates opened the carriage door.

He had flung out the box when they were passing a clump of bushes, which was the only type of vegetation which grew on the Plains.

It was unlikely, the Viscount thought, that it would ever be discovered.

If it was, it was doubtful if the discoverer would have the slightest idea to what use it had been put.

Another half-an-hour passed, and now there was a change.

There were trees, bushes, and even a few sheep to be seen near the railway.

It was now, the Viscount thought, the test came.

If, as he had suspected, Alexander III had telegraphed the Secret Police, they would be waiting for him.

He took off his coat and threw it over a chair.

He told Bates to bring him a cup of coffee and place it in front of him.

Bates had put the sofa back as it was when they had first joined the train.

He made the bed the Princess had used untidy, as if one person had slept in it.

The Viscount was giving a good impersonation of a man who had been resting.

There was no hurry to rush off the train until he was ready.

Bates moved all the luggage to the door.

When the train came to a standstill, he started to lift it down on to the platform.

He had taken three cases out of the carriage.

As he came back to pick up a fourth, he said out of the corner of his mouth:

"Here they come!"

The Viscount rose and started to put on his coat.

He was just pulling it across him, when three men, quite obviously Russians, came into the carriage.

One of them, who was in charge of the group, had a number of papers in his hands.

"Are you the Viscount Bredon?" he said in Russian, mispronouncing the name.

"I am," the Viscount replied.

"We have to search the carriage," the Russian said abruptly.

"Search away!" the Viscount replied. "I doubt if my Servant has left anything behind."

He moved towards the door, but the Russian stood in his way.

"Have you," he asked, "seen a young Lady while you have been in this train?"

The Viscount looked most convincingly surprised.

"A young Lady?" he replied. "I have seen no-one but my Servant."

"You are sure there has been no young Lady with you," the man repeated.

While he was speaking, the two other men had

gone into the bedroom and the Luggage-Room.

"I assure you there is no young Lady with me," the Viscount said. "Now I think a carriage is waiting for me. I wish to leave the Station."

Reluctantly the Russian moved because he could think of no way to stop him.

The men coming from the bedroom were shaking their heads to show there was no-one there.

The Viscount picked up his hat and stick which Bates had left on the chair and stepped on to the platform.

Bates, by this time, had managed to collect the trolley on which he had put the luggage.

He had also found a rather rough-looking Porter to pull it.

They set off down the platform, the Viscount moving apparently in no hurry.

He was looking around him as if he were interested in visiting a new place.

When he had reached the end of the platform, there were officials to inspect his passport.

They were, however, not concerned with him.

The Russians, by this time, were looking round at the other passengers who had been moving in the same direction as the Viscount.

Bates had gone ahead with the luggage.

When the Viscount came out from the Station, he saw an impressive-looking carriage, and sitting in the back seat was the Princess.

"I hopes yer don't mind, M'Lord," Bates said to the Viscount, "but this Lady, who be English, has not been met at th' Station as her expected. She asks my advice as to how her could proceed to the Hotel. I felt sure Yer Lordship'd be kind enough to give her a lift."

"Of course," the Viscount said, "naturally I am delighted."

He bent forward to shake hands with the Princess.

"I am sorry to hear you have been stranded," he said. "It is always difficult to get a carriage, unless one has ordered it beforehand."

"I thought mine had been," the Princess said. "It is very kind of your man to say you would take me as far as the Hotel."

"I am in no hurry," the Viscount said.

He sat down on the seat beside the Princess.

Bates climbed up to sit rather cramped between the Coachman and the Footman on the box.

As they drove off, the Princess slipped her hand into the Viscount's.

"We have ... done ... it! We have ... done it!" she whispered. "I have ... escaped. How can I ... ever thank ... you?"

"We are not out of the woods yet," the Viscount said almost in a whisper. "We must be very, very careful."

He did not add that the Third Section never gave up.

He was quite certain that the Princess was aware of this.

They drove through what was a quiet, pleasant street lined with trees.

There were a few shops, but it was quite obvious that Bistritz was not an important town.

They did not talk because the Viscount thought it was a mistake.

When they drew up outside a rather austere and not particularly attractive Hotel, the Princess said in a whisper:

"You will not drive away without waiting for me?"

The Viscount smiled.

"You must be aware by this time that I have realised that 'in for a penny, in for a pound.' "

She gave a little giggle but repressed it quickly.

She said in the same rather wavering old voice she had used before:

"You have been ... very kind to give ... me a ... lift."

"As it happens," the Viscount said, "I have

someone to meet here, so I would have come to this Hotel anyway."

He spoke so that the Servants on the box, if they understood English, would know what he was saying.

Then in Hungarian he repeated to them that he had someone to meet.

It would therefore be a short while before he could continue his journey.

Somewhat later, before he went into the Hotel, he asked the Coachman:

"Where am I staying?"

"With Baron Pressburg, M'Lord," the Coachman replied in Hungarian.

The Viscount raised his eyebrows.

This was something he had not expected.

He thought perhaps there was not the right sort of accommodation in Bistritz for him as a Representative of Great Britain.

Therefore the Hungarians, well known for their hospitality, had asked the Baron to accommodate him.

He wondered if it would make it more difficult when he had to introduce the Princess as his wife.

Then he told himself it was no use worrying.

He would just have to play it by instinct and hope for the best.

The "old Lady" vanished into the Hotel with Bates carrying her case.

By the time the Viscount was inside what he realised was the main hall, he saw the Princess and Bates going up the stairs.

He settled himself down in a comfortable chair and ordered a drink from an attentive Waiter.

He was wondering how he could account for the change in the Princess when she came back looking like herself.

It all seemed very complicated.

Yet he knew this was the only way they could have got away from the Russian Spies.

They would be wondering what they should do next.

The most important thing would be for them not to find out that he had suddenly produced a wife.

Then it struck him that it might be much easier to keep the Princess a secret if he was staying with Baron Pressburg, whoever he might be.

With any luck he would live outside the town rather than inside.

It was only a quarter-of-an-hour before the Princess came down the stairs with Bates behind her.

At a first glance the Viscount thought that she had not changed and looked exactly as she had when she left the train.

She came across the room towards him, and by this time there were several other people sitting at the small tables ordering drinks.

As she reached him he saw that once again Bates had been clever.

The Princess was wearing almost the same clothes in which she had left the train.

There was the veil over her face which had not disguised the dark lines of age under her eyes and round her mouth.

The veil was still there but the lines had gone, and so had the white hair.

As she sat down beside him with her back to the Reception Desk, the Viscount realised that once again they had diddled anyone who was spying on them.

"Bates engaged a room for me for half-an-hour," the Princess said, "so that I could freshen up before taking a long journey into the country."

As she spoke, the Viscount saw Bates at the Reception Desk paying for the room.

He got to his feet, saying:

"I think we should leave as quickly as possible."

"Yes, of course," the Princess agreed.

She rose too, and they left the Hotel just as some other people were coming in.

If anyone had been watching her, which was unlikely, they would not have been aware of how many years she had dropped between coming and going.

The carriage was waiting for them outside.

The Viscount helped the Princess in, leaving Bates to explain why they were taking another Lady with them.

He was aware that no ordinary person would have noticed that a pretty ribbon and a feather had been added to her hat.

She was wearing the same cloak, and yet, as she moved, there was a much younger, prettier dress underneath it.

What was clever, the Viscount thought, was that the veiling had been most appropriate both for the old and the new!

Actually he had to admit that with the hat retrimmed and tipped a little on one side, the veil was just as provocative as anything he had seen in Rotten Row.

The carriage drove off.

"Do you know where we are going?" the Princess asked.

"Apparently we are staying with a Baron of whom I have never heard," the Viscount replied. "I am just hoping that his house is well out of the town."

"I was hoping that myself," the Princess said. "I suddenly thought of something when I was dressing. We have not thought of a name for me. I can hardly be Yentha, for whom everybody is looking."

"I am aware of that," the Viscount said, although actually he had forgotten. "What would you like to be called?"

"I thought Tana was near enough. It is an abbreviation of my name, so I shall not forget it," the Princess said. "Or do you think it is not English enough?"

"I think actually Tana is Scottish," the Viscount replied, "and it would be a great mistake for you not to remember who you were. If we say your Father's name, we will have to make him English."

"That is quite easy," the Princess said. "My Mother, as you know, was a Thorpe, as her Father was the Duke of Wilthorpe. She can quite easily have married a Cousin, in which case, if I am asked, which I very much doubt, I was Tana Thorpe."

"That sounds excellent to me," the Viscount said, "and is something you will not easily forget."

"I hope not," the Princess said. "You must not let me talk too much, otherwise I am certain to make an awful gaffe and put my foot in it."

"Just remember that we met while I was in Russia and were married in St. Petersburg. It is far too complicated for anyone from here to make investigations—and why should they as far as we are concerned?"

"Of course! You are quite right! Why should they?" the Princess said. "Actually it is . . . very . . . exciting and once I am . . . in England I shall be safe for . . . ever and . . . ever."

The Viscount felt this was true.

At the same time, he could not help thinking they were still a very long way from home.

chapter three

THEY drove for two or three miles and were in the depth of the countryside.

The Viscount, who had been to Hungary before, always thought it was one of the most attractive countries he knew, or had ever seen.

The horses were superb.

He supposed there was no chance of him being able to ride while he was there.

He knew he must get to Budapest as quickly as possible, and then to on to Vienna.

After what the Princess had told him about Pandjeh, it was essential that he should be in touch with Lord Granville as soon as was humanly possible.

It would, however, not be wise to send a message that could be in any way decoded and understood by other people.

The Princess was looking at the trees and flowers as they drove past, and she said:

"I suppose you speak Hungarian."

"A little," the Viscount replied. "Magyar, as they call it here, is a very, very complicated language and the majority of the people speak either German, French, or occasionally Russian."

The Princess shivered.

"That is something I hope to avoid!"

53

"Of course," the Viscount said, "but I expect you will find our Host, if he is one of the Aristocrats, as he sounds, will speak English."

They drove on for a little longer and then saw ahead of them a very impressive-looking building.

It resembled in some ways a Castle.

Yet it had obviously been modernized and stood out from a background of trees.

The Viscount was wondering who Baron Pressburg was, and why they should be staying with him.

When they entered the house and were announced by an impressive *Major Domo*, an elderly man came hurrying down the room towards them.

"I am delighted to see you, My Lord," he said to the Viscount in very passable English, "and even more pleased that you should stay with me."

"It was a surprise to learn that you had been kind enough to invite me," the Viscount replied.

The elderly man chuckled.

"I thought it would be a surprise. Actually, your Ambassador should have been here to greet you, but he explained that he had very important business in Budapest and asked me to deputise for him."

"That was very kind of you," the Viscount said.

He was aware as he was speaking that the Baron kept glancing at the Princess.

He therefore said before the Baron could ask the questions:

"It must be a surprise to you that I am not alone. While I was in St. Petersburg I was married and therefore, as you can understand, I have brought my wife with me."

The Baron threw up his hands in a gesture of astonishment.

"Married!" he said. "This is certainly a very auspicious occasion. Of course, I am delighted to meet your wife."

He kissed the Princess's hand, and the Viscount said:

"My wife is English. In fact, you may have met her Grandfather, the Duke of Wilthorpe, and I am sure when you know her, you will agree that I am a very lucky man."

"Your wife is beautiful! Very beautiful!" the Baron said admiringly. "Of course I must drink to your health and happiness. Fortunately a bottle of Champagne was already waiting for you."

He moved towards a table in the corner of a very large room, where there was a bottle of Champagne in a gold ice-cooler.

When they each had a glass in their hands, the Baron raised his.

He said in Hungarian a Toast which the Viscount knew wished them a long life and happiness.

Then, when they sat down, the Baron said:

"I expect after such a long journey your wife would like to have a rest before dinner and, as I know you cannot stay with me for long, I have invited a number of people to meet you, all of whom are interested in the matters which concern us both."

The Viscount was aware of what he was implying, and he therefore said to the Princess:

"I am sure, my Dear, that you would like a little rest. We have come a long way, and the noise of the train is still rattling in our ears."

"That is true," the Princess said.

She had raised her veil to drink the Champagne, and the Viscount thought how lovely she looked.

He was aware by the expression in the Baron's eyes that he thought the same.

The *Major Domo* was ordered to take the Princess to the Housekeeper, and the Viscount and the Baron sat down.

As the door closed, the Baron said in a low voice:

"I am very eager to hear what you have discovered in St. Petersburg. There are very strange rumors going round this country as to what the Russians are doing in the East."

The Viscount had been thinking during the night that he would be wise not to disclose about the Tsar's ambitions if the countries he still had to visit were unaware of the havoc that the Ruler was creating.

"Things are certainly a little strained at the moment," he replied. "But I know that everyone in England is hoping they will not get worse."

He thought as he spoke that if the Princess was right—and he knew she was—they were certainly very much worse.

But it would be a mistake to say so.

The Baron sighed.

"Of course, as we border with Russia, we are in a very difficult position, and I understand that strange things are happening in the Balkans."

"That is true," the Viscount said. "But the Tsar kept assuring me that there was no need for Britain to be perturbed at his advance in the East."

The Baron frowned.

"The Russians invariably say one thing and do another," he said. "But you will understand it would be a mistake for me to say anything against them."

The Viscount understood this only too well.

He found it rather perturbing that someone like the Baron, who was obviously of importance in Hungary, should actually at this moment be afraid of the Tsar.

"Well, we can talk about it tonight," the Baron said. "I know my friends will be grateful for anything encouraging you could tell them. We are all, as you can understand, very apprehensive."

They drank a little more Champagne.

Then, as time was getting on, the Viscount went upstairs.

He was shown into the bedroom, where the Princess was resting.

"Your Dressing-Room is next door," the Baron said, "and Dinner is at eight o'clock. A little late, but some of our Guests have to come from a long distance."

The Viscount thanked him and then, as he shut the door, moved across the room.

There was a very large and comfortable bed under a carved gold canopy.

The Princess was lying down.

"What is happening?" she asked.

"Nothing in particular," the Viscount answered.

"Your Dressing-Room is next door."

"That is what I have been told," he answered.

"It has a small, rather uncomfortable bed in it, and it is only fair that that is where I should sleep tonight, and you can have this one."

The Viscount laughed.

"I will not deprive you. May I say the curtains and the canopy of gold are a perfect frame for your beauty."

It was the sort of compliment he would have paid any other woman he was with.

But the Princess exclaimed:

"Now you are making me conceited, and after what you have said, I shall certainly want to sleep here!"

"I am only thankful," the Viscount said, "that I have a bed at all. We cannot expect Bates to alter the sofas in a Private House."

The Princess laughed.

"I am sure that he would prevent you from sleeping on the floor," she said. "Thank you for saying that I may keep my golden frame."

The Viscount walked to the connecting room which led into the Dressing-Room.

He was thinking as he did so that only the Princess would have made the fact that he was seeing her in bed for the first time quite so easy.

He knew any other woman would have either been very seductive, or else, if she was as young as the Princess, shy and embarrassed.

Instead, she behaved exactly as she had on the train, as if, he repeated to himself, I were her brother or her Father.

Bates was waiting for him in the Dressing-Room.

It had a large and important-looking wardrobe and a writing-desk as well as several inlaid chests which the Viscount knew were unique.

The bed, as the Princess had said, was not very impressive.

The Viscount thought that certainly it would not have been much used in the past.

"Well, here we are, M'Lord," Bates said. "It looks to me more comfortable to what we might 'ave expected."

"I agree with you," the Viscount said.

"I've a bath ready for Yer Lordship," Bates went on, "and I thinks you needs it after that train journey."

"I do indeed," the Viscount replied.

He had his bath and felt fresher and cooler than he had felt for the last three days.

Bates told him it had been arranged with the Housemaids that they would carry in the bath for the Princess.

When he looked at the clock, the Viscount saw it was getting on for Dinner time.

He was, in fact, just putting on his evening-coat, when there was a knock on the door.

To his surprise, when Bates opened it, he saw it was the Baron.

"We are nearly ready," the Viscount said.

"I want a word with you in private, My Lord," the Baron said.

He was speaking English.

Bates immediately went into the Bathroom and shut the door.

The Baron waited for a moment, and then he said in a low voice:

"I have something to tell you which you may find rather uncomfortable."

"What is it?" the Viscount asked.

"I have just had a message from Count Odoevsky, who is Russian."

The Viscount stiffened, but he did not speak.

"He has heard of your arrival," the Baron went on, "and he has asked if he, and a man who is always with him, can come to Dinner to meet you."

There was a pause before the Viscount said:

"I presume it is impossible for you to refuse?"

"Quite impossible!" the Baron said. "Unless I make things more difficult than they are at the moment."

He threw out his hands in a very eloquent gesture as he added:

"What can I do? What can I say? Of course the Count was aware that the people I have asked tonight all feel as I do about the continual Russian infiltration into this country, just as they are infiltrating into all the others."

The Viscount had guessed that was the real reason he had arranged the Dinner, and he said:

"It is certainly very disappointing!"

"I thought that was what you would feel, My Lord, but there is nothing I can do but pretend the evening is just a Social occasion."

He gave a deep sigh before he added:

"They are making life for me, and a great number of other people, absolutely impossible."

The Viscount was thinking quickly, then he said:

"There is one thing which is very important, and that is that the Russians should not know I am married."

The Baron looked surprised.

"I thought you told me you were married in St. Petersburg?"

"Actually that is not true," the Viscount replied. "My wife met me here to join me on my homeward journey. For reasons I need not go into, ours has been a secret marriage, and we wanted to be alone together before it was announced publicly in the British newspapers."

The Baron smiled.

"I can see that is very romantic," he said, "and I can understand you not wanting the Russians to know of your marriage before your own people."

"As my wife's family are so important in England, it would cause a great deal of disagreeableness if the news that we were man and wife reached them before we had told them ourselves that we have made a runaway match."

"I understand! Of course I understand!" the Baron exclaimed. "My dear boy, I congratulate you more than I have done already. Your wife is beautiful. One of the most beautiful women I have ever seen. Of course you were right to marry her, whatever the opposition."

"You are very kind," the Viscount said. "Now, if you will permit me, I will tell my wife that she is to stay in her room and have Dinner there. Your Guests, and, of course, the Russians, need have no idea that she is in the house."

He could see that the Baron was delighted with the intrigue.

It was just the sort of tale the romantic Hungarians would enjoy.

"My Guests will suffer," the Baron said, "because they will not have the honor and delight of meeting anyone so lovely. But I promise she shall have a delicious Dinner."

"Ask your Servants not to talk to the Russian Servants," the Viscount said. "You know how they would relish the idea that she was hiding from them."

"Yes, of course. I can trust my Servants, who have been with me for a long time. The majority of them loathe the Russians, and what they are doing to this country."

The Baron walked towards the door and went out.

The Viscount quickly knocked on the communicating door to the Princess's bedroom.

When she said: "Come in!" he saw she was sitting at the Dressing-Table.

One of the Maids was pinning a rose into her hair.

As she turned round to look at him, he thought that no-one could be so lovely.

The Baron was right when he said it was a loss for his Guests that they should not see her.

"I wish to speak to my wife alone!" the Viscount said in Hungarian to the Maid, who quickly left the room.

"What is it? What has happened?" the Princess asked as the door shut.

"Two Russians," the Viscount answered, "who apparently terrify the Baron and the neighbourhood, have invited themselves to Dinner."

The Princess gave a cry of horror.

"Russians! Then they . . . know I . . . am . . . here."

"I do not think they have the slightest idea of that," the Viscount said. "What they do know is that our Host has invited a number of people who are extremely perturbed at the Russians' behavior in this country. They are therefore determined that they shall not intrigue with me or let me carry information to England of which they do not approve."

The Princess gave a deep sigh.

"They are everywhere! How can anybody possibly allow them to go on in this . . . disgraceful . . . manner?"

The Viscount did not give the obvious answer.

Russia was too big and too powerful for any country to attack her single-handed.

Instead, he said:

"I have now told the Baron that we were not married in St. Petersburg as I had said at first, but we have had a secret marriage which is not approved of by your relations."

The Princess was listening wide-eyed.

"We are spending a little time together," the Viscount explained, "on my way home, before we face

the music, when we do arrive, from those who dis-
approve of our marriage."

The Princess clapped her hands.

"Now you are being very clever and no longer
stuffy! I like you when you are imaginative."

"Thank you!" the Viscount said. "As I have told
you before, I dislike telling lies, but there is nothing
else I could do at this moment."

He looked at the rose in her hair, and said:

"Now you are all dressed up with nowhere to go.
The poor Baron is devastated that you are not there
to entrance his visitors."

"If they include two Russians, then it is something
to be avoided at all costs," the Princess said.

"The Baron has promised you a delicious Dinner,
but unfortunately you must eat it here."

The Princess looked up at him for a moment.

"You must be very, very careful not to let them
know that I am with you. If they are at all suspicious,
they will . . . find me . . . however . . . hard I try to . . .
hide from . . . them."

"Now you are being defeatist," the Viscount said.
"We have been very clever so far, and there is no
reason why we should fail now."

Because he wished to reassure her and saw she was
frightened, he said:

"It is a challenge. Quite frankly, I am determined
to beat the Russians and get you to England safely."

The Princess threw out her arms.

"That is exactly what I want you to do! Now you
are no longer pompous, saying how you could never
tell a lie, even to save me!"

"I imagine I will be telling a great number before
we finally set foot on English soil," the Viscount said.
"If I have to lie, I prefer it to be a good one."

"I am sure if you will give it your full attention, it
will be a very, very good one," the Princess said.

"We ought to be grateful that we have been warned
in advance about these Russians. If I had walked un-

expectedly downstairs, it might have been into a hornets' nest."

She shuddered as she spoke, and the Viscount said:

"You will be quite safe up here. The Baron is telling his Servants to be very careful what they say. Apparently they dislike the Russians as much as he does."

The Princess took the rose out of her hair.

"I will just go back to bed," she said. "At least it is a very comfortable one."

She gave a little sideways glance before she added:

"Are you quite sure you do not want to change places with me?"

"You are being sensible and very brave," the Viscount said, "and although it will be a silent toast, I will drink to you when I am downstairs."

He took her hand and raised it to his lips in the same way as the Baron had done.

"I will not wake you when I come to bed," he said, "unless there is something very important you should know before tomorrow."

He continued:

"I am going to suggest to the Baron that we leave very early in the morning, before the Russians have any idea we are going. In fact, I shall go out of my way this evening to say that we might stay another night."

"Now you are being as shrewd as they are," the Princess said, "and I must thank you for worrying about me."

"Ever since the night you arrived in your black box," the Viscount said, "I had little choice."

She smiled at him.

Then he hurried back to his own room to tell Bates what was happening.

"I'll keep an eye on 'em downstairs," Bates said.

"We must leave on the first train to Budapest," the Viscount said. "Find out what time it goes and get the

Major Domo to order a carriage for us." ·

"I'll see to it, M'Lord," Bates replied. "And what yer 'ave to do is to get them Ruskies so drunk that when they wakes up in th' morning they'll not know if it's Christmas or Easter."

"That is certainly an idea," the Viscount said reflectively.

"I thinks if I tips the Head Butler," Bates said, "and I have never known a foreigner who'll not take money, he might mix the wine an' of course see them Ruskies never have an empty glass."

"You do that," the Viscount said.

He took a large note from the case in which he kept money ready for each country he was visiting, and handed it to Bates.

He knew it was well spent.

He was sure that the Russians, who were noticeably hard drinkers, would be staggering when they finally left.

When he went downstairs, it was to find that a number of the Guests had already arrived.

They were all obviously eager to meet him.

As the Russians were not there, practically every man to whom he was introduced said:

"I hear that our evening has been spoilt. It does not surprise me. But Your Lordship is now aware of what we are having to put up with in this part of the world."

"I am very sorry for you," the Viscount said.

He was even more sorry when Count Odoevsky was announced with his friend, who was also a Count.

He had learnt in St. Petersburg there were over a million Counts in Russia.

He was not therefore impressed by their titles, nor by the Russian themselves.

Count Odoevsky was a hard-faced man with narrow eyes which had an Oriental touch about them.

He had the tight, straight lips and square chin of a Russian bully.

His friend was even more sinister.

The Viscount thought that if he had to choose a picture of two men who were obviously part of the Third Section, they would have been perfect examples.

It was obvious from the moment they arrived that the tempo fell.

The Hungarians, who were talking in their usual good-humored way on every subject and making each other laugh, lapsed into silence.

They dined in a large Banqueting-Room at a table groaning with gold plates.

It would have been obvious to any onlooker that something was wrong.

It was impossible to have a conversation on the subject which concerned the Viscount and was the reason they were there.

They therefore talked about horses and kept off politics.

The Russians, however, tried to draw the Viscount out about his experiences in St. Petersburg.

He guessed they hoped he would be indiscreet, in which case he would be reported immediately to the Tsar.

Instead, he praised St. Petersburg.

He eulogised about the beauty of the Winter Palace and the pictures and other treasures that could be seen there.

He realised he was annoying the Russians, but there was nothing they could do about it.

He was delighted to see, as the Dinner progressed, they were drinking more and more.

They had only to sip from a glass to have it refilled by one of the Servants.

At last, the excellent Dinner, with a great number of courses, came to an end.

It was then the Brandy and other liqueurs were taken round the table.

The Viscount was watching Count Odoevsky.

He saw a glass put beside him which was filled to the brim.

The Count drank it in the same way that the Russians always drank Vodka.

They did not taste it, but as the Viscount himself said, "chucked it down their throats."

Whatever the glass contained, it certainly did what he had hoped it would do.

The Russian flung it over his shoulder so that it smashed on the ground behind him.

Then he collapsed slowly while the rest of the Guests watched him.

First he slipped down on to his chair, and from there on to the floor.

His Russian friend rose unsteadily to go to his assistance.

The Servants carried him, apparently unconscious, out of the room.

His friend followed him.

There was absolute silence until the door had closed.

When those left behind were quite certain the Russians were out of hearing, they laughed.

They laughed uncontrollably, as if they could not help themselves, and the tears came into their eyes.

Even the Viscount had to admit it was very funny.

He was certain that Bates was at the bottom of the joke.

"Now we can talk," the Baron said in a tone of satisfaction.

"Do you think it is safe?" one of his Guests asked.

"Are you suggesting that they have a listening post in the house?" the Baron enquired. "That is impossible, as we are all aware what happened last year, so I assure you every precaution has been taken."

The Viscount was to learn later than the Russians

had somehow clandestinely listened in the house of an important Hungarian Nobleman who was noted for expressing his opinion.

He had every reason to dislike his Russian neighbours.

He had, however, gone too far.

When he was out riding, he had an unfortunate accident which nobody saw, in which he broke his neck.

It was this sort of story, and a great many others, which the Viscount heard as they sat round the table until after midnight.

When the Guests left, they all said how much they had enjoyed meeting him.

It was then he told the Baron that it was essential he and his wife should leave as early as possible the next morning.

"There is a train to Budapest at seven o'clock," the Baron said. "I cannot believe that the Count will be on his feet by that time."

"I would be surprised if he stirs before mid-day," the Viscount replied.

The Baron had spoken to his Butler as the last of the Guests were departing.

He said now:

"I understand, My Lord, it was your Valet's idea that we should, in English parlance, 'lace his wine.' I suppose it was stupid of me, but it was something I had never though of myself."

"It can be very effective," the Viscount said.

"It was a brilliant idea, and very well carried out," the Baron said. "It would be difficult for him to accuse me of attacking him in any way. I can hardly be responsible for what he drinks."

"I am sure you will be worried tomorrow, in case he is not feeling well," the Viscount said.

"Of course," the Baron agreed. "I will send a Servant to enquire if he is better and say how deeply grieved we all were that he had to leave us so early."

The two men laughed.

Then the Baron put his hand on the Viscount's shoulder.

"You were very helpful and very encouraging to us tonight," he said. "Personally I find it difficult to see an end to this intolerable position which can only get worse, not better."

The Viscount felt the same, but he did not say so.

He merely answered:

"Thank you for being so kind to me and my wife. We shall never forget your kindness. I hope if you ever come to England, you will stay with us."

"I am getting too old to move about much at my age," the Baron said, "but if you ever get the chance, come here and ride my horses. I know you are an outstanding rider, and I can assure you that I have in my Stables Hungary's best."

"It is agonising for me to have to leave without seeing them," the Viscount said, "but thank you, and I promise, if I get the opportunity to come back, I will let you know."

They shook hands, and the Viscount went up to his room.

He went in very quietly.

He had told Bates not to wait up for him because he knew the man had so much to do in getting the luggage ready and arranging for them to leave so early.

The Viscount took off his coat.

He was just undoing his tie, when the communicating door opened and the Princess came in.

"What has happened?" she asked.

" I thought you would be asleep," the Viscount replied.

"How could I sleep, thinking that perhaps at any moment those men might guess I was here and come upstairs to search for me?"

"You are quite safe," the Viscount said.

She was standing in the doorway with the light behind her.

She was wearing only a soft woollen shawl over her shoulders.

Her nightgown was diaphanous, and the outline of her slim body was very evident.

"Go on into bed," the Viscount said, "and I will come to tell you exactly what has happened."

She did as he told her.

He took off his waistcoat.

Then, wearing just a shirt and trousers, he went into her room.

He found himself thinking that they could quite easily be a husband and wife who had been married for some years.

They were, therefore, quite used to seeing each other only partially dressed.

'Can this really be happening to me?' he wondered.

He thought what his friends who had told him he was a *Roué* and a womanizer would say.

They would never believe for one moment that there was nothing between him and the Princess but the difficulty of saving her from the Tsar of Russia.

She was sitting up in bed when he reached her.

The lights on the table beside it made her look even more glamorous than she had been when he had first seen her under the great gold canopy.

It also revealed the soft curves of her breasts.

Her skin was almost dazzlingly white in contrast to her dark hair which fell over her shoulders.

The Viscount reminded himself that he was there to explain to her what had happened at Dinner.

He told her how unpleasant the Russians were.

Every one of the Baron's Guests, when they left, had a story to tell of their interference and their cruelty.

There was a number of murders which could not be accounted for.

"Poor people! I am so sorry for them!" the Princess exclaimed. "But what can you do about it?"

"I can only report to London on what is happening," the Viscount answered. "I am convinced that sooner or later, if we do not fight Russia in the East, we will have to fight here in Europe."

He was surprised at the strength and firmness of his own words.

It was as if they came to his lips, not through his own volition, but through a Power greater than himself.

"A War would be disastrous," he said quickly. "But what else would have any effect?"

"Now tell me what is happening to us?" the Princess said as if she must get back to the reality of the moment.

"We will leave here at six o'clock tomorrow morning," the Viscount said, "and that is why I hoped you would be asleep."

"Do you think the Russians will be suspicious if we leave so early?"

"They were sober when I told them I was looking forward to riding the Baron's magnificent horses," the Viscount said. "There are no horses in the world as good as those in Hungary."

"Were they impressed?" the Princess asked.

"They were trying all the time to trip me up in some way. I think that was because they had nothing concrete to go on but knew instinctively that something was wrong."

His voice was serious as he went on:

"We must be very, very careful, you and I, and I must remember to call you Tana and to assert, as I did tonight to the Baron, that you are entirely English."

"He is such a nice man," the Princess said. "I am sorry that he cannot learn the truth."

The Viscount held up his hand.

"That is wrong thinking. We must convince ourselves that you are English. There is not one drop of Russian blood in your veins."

He spoke so firmly, the Princess said humbly:

"I am . . . sorry! You told . . . me to . . . think right . . . and I . . . have been . . . trying."

"You have done very well so far," the Viscount said. "We cannot let those extremely unpleasant men beat us."

"No! Of course not," the Princess agreed. "Thank you . . . thank you for being . . . so sensible and so very . . . clever."

She gave him a fascinating little smile before she added:

"Was I not clever to find you and Bates?"

"You must congratulate Bates tomorrow," the Viscount said. "Now I am going to bed. He will call you and me at five-thirty, because it would be a mistake to let too many of the household know what is happening."

"I will be ready," the Princess said. "One of my virtues is that I am invariably punctual."

Moving towards the connecting door, the Viscount thought he had seen a great number of other virtues as well.

He turned back to wave to her before he left the room.

He thought as he did so that she made a picture that any man of any age would find entrancing.

Then he told himself he had no intention of being emotionally involved with a young woman who had pushed herself onto him any more than he intended to be married to her or to anyone else.

"Tonight just shows," he told himself as he undressed, "for someone on a Diplomatic Mission to have a wife is a terrible mistake!"

He sighed and continued:

"Here am I, involved in an absolute quagmire of lies, and there are still three countries in which I have to repeat them before I can become a bachelor again."

He threw his clothes down on a chair and got into bed.

It was quite comfortable and he was tired.

At the same time, he could not help seeing the picture the Princess had made in the gold-canopied bed.

The Viscount felt that he had only shut his eyes for a few minutes before Bates was beside him.

"Time to get up, M'Lord," he said. "Everything's arranged. If we miss this train, there ain't another one 'til mid-day."

That spurred the Viscount as nothing else would have done.

By the time he had dressed he was aware that the Princess was ready too.

She was wearing the same clothes in which she had arrived, with a veil over her face.

The Viscount tipped the Servants generously.

He knew the Russians, following the example of the Tsar, were extremely mean when it came to tips.

The carriage was waiting for them outside, but there was no sign of their host.

The *Major Domo* explained that he bade them "*bon voyage*."

But he felt that they would understand that as an old man he found it difficult to get up early in the morning.

"Of course my wife and I understand," the Viscount said. "Will you tell him how deeply grateful we are for his hospitality and how well we have been looked after by his staff."

The *Major Domo* appreciated this.

He bowed very low as they drove away.

It was a great relief to find there was no-one at the Station who looked at them suspiciously.

They were, however, on a different platform to the one on which they arrived.

This was for interior travel and not so important.

The men who put the luggage into the train were interested only in the *pourboire* they would receive from the Viscount.

The train fortunately started from here and was therefore on time.

The first part of the journey was extremely slow, as the train stopped to pick up quite a number of goods that went to market.

It was only when they were out of the Bistritz area that the engine really started to move.

Then, with a sense of relief, the Viscount admitted they had got away.

When the Russians were aware of it, there was nothing they could do.

"Once we are in Budapest, we shall be under the protection of the British Embassy," he said aloud.

"I was thinking more or less the same thing," the Princess answered.

She was taking off her dark cape.

She followed it with her hat and veil and threw them down on the seat beside her.

"You have to admit," she said, "we have been lucky so far."

"We still have a long way to go," the Viscount replied.

"Now you are being an old gloom again," she retorted. "I was thinking last night how extremely lucky we have been, and thank goodness those ghastly Russians did not just spring a surprise on the Baron."

"I agree with you that that was extremely lucky," the Viscount said. "But we are still in Hungary and they might telegraph their suspicions to the quite large number of Spies who are lurking in Budapest."

"I refuse to anticipate the worst," the Princess said. "So look happy! I think what you really need is a glass of Champagne."

"Have we got any?" the Viscount enquired.

"I am quite certain that the Baron thought of it. If not, Bates would have," the Princess replied.

Of course she was right.

There was Champagne standing in the bowl which contained ice that was beginning to melt.

The Viscount opened the bottle.

"I suppose you know it is considered quite outrageously fast," he said, "for anyone to be drinking Champagne before breakfast."

"We get that at the next stop," the Princess said. "I think Bates thought we scarcely had time to catch our breath before we caught the train."

The Viscount laughed.

"Bates always knows best!" he said.

He lifted his glass, saying:

"To a remarkably intelligent and very punctual young woman!"

The Princess raised hers.

"To an English Gentleman," she said softly.

chapter four

IT was getting on for half-past eight before the train
began to slow down for its first stop.

"I am hungry," the Princess said, "so I do hope we
get a good breakfast."

"I am sure Bates has discovered that it is the best
Restaurant on the line," the Viscount replied, "and we
could hardly ask for a large meal before we left."

"I think the Hungarian food, as a whole, is very
good," the Princess said. "Last night's Dinner, although I had to eat it alone, was delicious."

"I thought of you," the Viscount answered, "while
those ghastly Russians were making everybody de-
pressed and the Hungarians almost silent."

The Princess laughed.

"They love talking! I remember when they used to
visit us in St. Petersburg, Papa and Mama could hardly get a word in."

There was a soft look in her eyes which the Viscount knew was invariably there when she spoke of
her Parents.

The train came to a standstill.

Bates, who was in the next carriage, opened the
door.

"I'm going to get yer breakfast, M'Lord," he said.
"Is there anything yer particularly fancy?"

"Anything that will taste good!" the Viscount replied.

"I suppose," the Princess said as Bates hurried away, "it would have been easier if we had gone to the Restaurant ourselves."

"It would be a mistake to leave the carriage together," the Viscount answered.

She gave him a quick glance and exclaimed:

"I had forgotten that we were . . . still on . . . dangerous ground."

"We must be very careful," he said. "It would be a mistake to be seen walking about until we are safely the other side of Europe."

The Princess nodded.

The Viscount was aware there was a touch of fear in her eyes.

He thought perhaps it was rather cruel to keep reminding her of their position.

At the same time, after what he had heard last night, he knew they should take no chances.

The Princess, who was looking out of the window, exclaimed:

"Here is Bates coming back quicker than I expected. I hope he has got something delicious for both of us."

The Viscount opened the door.

Then, as Bates stepped in with a tray in his hand, he said:

"Them two Russians as examined yer carriage, M'Lord, when us arrived are on th' platform. They're talking to the Guard!"

There was hardly a moment's pause before the Viscount said sharply:

"Pull down the blinds!"

He looked up at the luggage-rack.

Without saying anything, he picked the Princess up in his arms.

He deposited her in the rack, saying as he did so: "Lie down!"

He put her hat beside her and covered her completely with her black cape which was lying on the seat.

Then he picked up his own hat and put it on top of the Princess together with his walking-stick.

By this time Bates had pulled down all the blinds on each side of the carriage.

It was different to the one in which they had travelled from Russia.

In fact, it was an ordinary carriage with seats on either side.

Being First Class, they were padded and comfortable.

It was not up-to-date enough to have a corridor.

The Viscount had told Bates to find himself a seat in the next carriage.

He had noticed, because it was so early in the morning, that there was hardly anyone else travelling First Class.

Now, having had a last look at the Princess, the Viscount lay down on the seat.

He stretched out his legs and shut his eyes.

He had only just done so, when the door of the carriage opened.

The Viscount had not even spoken to Bates, except to tell him to pull down the blinds.

Seeing him with closed eyes told the little man exactly what to do.

He stood in the doorway, making it impossible for anyone to enter, and put his finger to his lips.

The Guard, who was accompanied by the two Russians, stared at him in surprise.

" 'Is Lordship's asleep!" Bates whispered. "An' yer don't want to wake him."

The Russians pushed forward to look into the carriage, but Bates did not move out of the doorway.

The Guard, who seemed rather nonplussed, said in Hungarian:

"I think these gentlemen wanted to speak to whoever's in here."

Bates did not understand. He merely said:

"I'm English, if that's wot yer asking me?"

The elder Russian pushed further forward, saying:

"Let me get into the carriage."

"What for?" Bates enquired. "An' keep yer voice down!"

The Russian peered round Bates.

It was obvious there was nothing to see except the Viscount, who did not move.

The breakfast tray lay on the opposite seat.

The Russian stepped back and had a word with his companion, who shrugged his shoulders.

Reluctantly, they appeared to admit to each other that there was nothing they could do.

They moved still further away.

Bates said to the Guard:

"Lock us in."

He demonstrated with his hands what he wanted.

He also slipped some coins into the Guard's hand.

The Guard understood.

With a backward glance at the Russians in case they should prevent it, he shut the door and turned the key in the lock.

As the blinds were down, Bates could not see what was happening.

After a few seconds the Viscount opened his eyes.

"That was clever of you, Bates," he said. "Have they gone away?"

"I thinks they've given up fer a moment, M'Lord," Bates replied. "It's lucky I sees them."

"Very lucky indeed," the Viscount said, sitting up.

The Princess peeped down at them from above.

"Can I come down?" she asked.

"Not until the train moves out of the Station," the Viscount replied. "We are locked in, but I think you will be safer where you are for the moment."

He then looked rather doubtfully at the breakfast-tray.

"That's all right, M'Lord," Bates said before he

asked the question. "I didn't want yer to hurry over what yer eating. I pays extra an' told them we'd leave the tray at the next stop."

"I can always trust you to think of everything in an emergency," the Viscount said.

At that moment they heard the Guard blow his whistle, and the train began to move.

"Look out, and tell me what those Russians are doing," the Viscount said sharply, "but do not let them see you!"

It was obviously a rather difficult request, but Bates managed just to peep out of the bottom of one of the blinds.

"They be standing in the centre of the platform, M'Lord, looking sour," he said. "Not that they ever looks anything else."

"Thank Heaven we left them behind," the Viscount replied. "I was afraid they might travel on the train with us."

He reached up and pulled the cape off the Princess.

"Now you can come down," he said.

He lifted her on to the seat and saw that she was looking rather pale.

"I suppose," she said in a low voice, "I was rather stupid not to anticipate that they might be still looking for me."

"It is something I should have anticipated," the Viscount said. "We can only be very grateful that Bates saw them before they came to the carriage and found you here."

"You are quite certain they have not got into the train?" the Princess asked Bates.

He shook his head.

"No, Yer Highness. Them were too far back on th' platform to have jumped in as we left."

"Now, do not worry about them," the Viscount said soothingly. "We are leaving them behind, and I am sure that once we are out of Hungary things will be far easier."

"I hope so," the Princess murmured.

They ate their breakfast which was surprisingly good. So was the coffee that Bates had brought them.

The Valet made himself as scarce as possible.

He sat at the other end of the carriage and looked out of the window at the country through which they were passing.

The Viscount offered him something to eat.

But he refused, saying that he had his breakfast at the Castle.

He had helped himself in the kitchen before he had gone upstairs to call them.

The train was soon moving very fast.

The Princess began to feel they were running towards safety.

The suspicious, unpleasant Russians had really been left behind.

There was only one more stop before, very late in the afternoon, they reached Budapest.

By that time both the Princess and Viscount felt they were left with little to say.

They dozed a little on either side of the carriage.

The Station in Budapest was very impressive.

At first sight it seemed overwhelmingly full of passengers.

The Viscount realised later that a large number of them were merely spectators.

Having nothing better to do, they enjoyed watching the trains and were also admirers of the Station itself.

Bates collected the baggage.

While they were waiting for him to do so, an elderly man came hurrying onto the platform.

He was looking at those he passed as if he were searching for someone.

The Viscount saw him first and went forward.

He had known Count Janos Moricz when he was Hungarian Ambassador in London.

He was delighted when Lord Granville had told

him that was who he would be staying with in Budapest.

The Count threw up his arms with excitement when the Viscount went towards him.

"My dear boy, here you are at last! I was afraid that something might have prevented you from reaching me."

"No! Here I am," the Viscount said. "It is delightful to see you again."

"My carriage is outside," the Count said, "and my Servant will see to your luggage."

He would have turned round.

The Viscount put out his hand to prevent him doing so.

"I am not alone!" he said.

Because there was such a crowd moving round them, Count Moricz had not noticed the Princess.

Now the Viscount said:

"This may surprise you, but my wife is with me!"

"Your wife!" Count Moricz exclaimed. "I had no idea you were married."

"I must tell you all about it," the Viscount said. "But let me introduce you."

He turned to the Princess.

"Yentha, this is a very old and dear friend of mine, Count Moricz, who was the Hungarian Ambassador in London for some years."

The Count kissed the Princess's hand.

Then, when they had seated themselves in his large and comfortable carriage, he said:

"It is a great privilege for me to entertain you, My Lord, and your beautiful wife. I cannot understand why none of the people who write to me from London told me that such a popular and eligible bachelor as yourself had finally been taken to the altar."

The Viscount laughed.

"They did not tell you because they did not know! We have been married secretly and have not yet broken the news to our families."

"A run-away marriage!" the Count exclaimed. "Now, that is very exciting. You must tell me all about it and why you were not married at St. George's in Hanover Square with a huge reception to follow it."

"That was one thing I was thankful to avoid," the Viscount said. "You may have enjoyed them while you were in England, but I find that sort of party exceedingly boring!"

He spoke lightly, and the Count laughed.

"You have always been different, My Lord, in what you say and what you do! As you can imagine, I am longing to hear what you thought of St. Petersburg."

Now, the Viscount thought, they were getting down to business.

That, at any rate, would keep the Count off being too inquisitive about his private affairs.

The Count's house was not very large but it was very comfortable.

It was obvious from his possessions that he was a rich man.

When the Princess had been taken upstairs, the Count took the Viscount into his Study.

The inevitable bottle of Champagne was waiting for them.

"I hope," he said, "that your wife will not find it too boring this evening, because I have invited a number of special friends who wish to meet you."

The Viscount knew exactly what this meant, and answered:

"My wife fully appreciates that I am here on business which concerns Lord Granville. If you would rather she did not join us for Dinner, she will understand."

"She will look like a jewel," the Count said. "At the same time, I am afraid she will find the conversation rather boring."

The Viscount agreed.

It would be the same conversation he had had in

the Baron's house last night after the Russians had left.

However, this was the reason why he was in Hungary.

He would have to listen to them saying over and over again how much they resented the Russian intrusion.

What was important was that he would get the Princess out of Hungary as soon as possible.

He hoped by now, having left the Russians many miles behind, they would not be a menace.

At the same time, the Princess would not be safe until they were in a very different part of Europe.

He talked to the Count until it was time for them both to go up to change for Dinner.

The bedrooms upstairs were very much the same as what they had with the Baron.

There was one very large impressive bedroom, and a rather austere Dressing-Room.

Fortunately, as the Viscount saw at a quick glance, it contained a bed.

"I do hope you will be comfortable," the Count said.

"I should not expect to be anything else in your house," the Viscount answered, "and also enjoy the most delicious food. I have not forgotten the Dinner-Parties you gave in London."

The old man was delighted at the compliment.

"I suppose," he said, "you have to leave tomorrow? There are a great number of other people here who would like to meet you besides those who will be dining with us tonight."

The Viscount shook his head.

"They will be waiting for us in Vienna," he replied, "and after that we have to go to Paris. My schedule has been very carefully thought out."

The Count laughed.

"That is certainly something you must not upset."

He was turning away, then stopped.

"Oh, by the way," he said, "as you tell me you have been married secretly, I suppose you have brought your Marriage Certificate with you."

The Viscount raised his eyebrows.

"I expect so!" he said vaguely. "But why should it be required?"

The Count lowered his voice as he answered:

"It is the Russians! Is there any other reason for all these new rules and regulations?"

"What are you saying?" the Viscount asked. "How does that concern a Marriage Certificate?"

"It is like this," the Count replied. "There were Russians passing through Hungary and into Austria who, as the Officials found, were there only to stir up trouble."

The Viscount knew this had happened in all the Balkan States.

"The Emperor," the Count went on, "therefore made it more difficult for the Russians by insisting that they had a job waiting for them or they were genuine travellers."

"I can understand that was necessary," the Viscount said.

"Then we had an influx of young women," the Count continued. "They had, of course, been trained by the Russians to obtain information from every man they met."

The Viscount sighed.

This was another thing he had been told last night.

Some of the tragedies which had occurred in consequence had been heart-breaking.

"So the Austrians now insist," the Count continued, "that if a pretty woman comes in with a man saying they are husband and wife, they have to show a Marriage Certificate."

The Viscount stiffened.

"Surely," he said, "it does not concern someone like myself, who holds a Diplomatic Passport?"

"You will find that you will have to endure a long

questioning as to why the woman you call your wife is with you. Several of my friends have missed their train in consequence."

The Viscount thought quickly.

"The more I think about it," he said, "I am convinced our Marriage Certificate was left behind in England."

He paused and then added almost pleadingly:

"Surely you can provide me with one? It would be terribly inconvenient if we missed the train to Vienna tomorrow, and I shall be rebuked for not having anticipated that this sort of thing might happen."

The Count smiled.

"We cannot have you in trouble, my dear boy. I will provide you with a Marriage Certificate even though it is rather short notice."

"If you can do that, I would be extremely grateful," the Viscount replied.

The Count walked across the room to the small *secrétaire* which was placed conveniently near the window.

He drew a piece of writing-paper from a leather case and picked up a pen.

"Now," he said, "give me both your names."

As he spoke, the communicating-door to the Princess's bedroom opened, and she came in.

"I can hear you talking," she said, "and I wondered what I was missing."

"What you are missing," the Viscount replied, "is that I have been very lax and left our Marriage Certificate behind which the Count tells me has to be shown tomorrow when we cross into Austria."

"Oh, dear! How tiresome!" the Princess exclaimed. "I expect it is my fault, but I did not think anyone would want to see it."

"Then your excuse is the same as mine," the Viscount said.

He thought she had been very quick in understanding the situation.

He thought, too, that she was looking very pretty.

She was already half dressed, in a lace-trimmed petticoat, which was covered by a light chiffon *négligée*.

Her hair had been arranged, the Viscount thought, by one of the Maids.

There were flowers at the back of it, not a rose like last night, but small orchids which looked like stars against her dark hair.

"Now, there is no need for you two to worry," the Count said. "Just give me your names, and there will be no difficulties tomorrow when you reach the frontier."

"I was christened Lyle Nicholas Henry," the Viscount said.

The Count wrote them down.

"And yours?" he said to the Princess.

Without thinking she said:

"Yentha."

She then realised she had made a mistake and looked at the Viscount.

He shook his head as if to tell her not to make a fuss and she went on quickly:

"Elizabeth Mary!"

"Now, what I will do," the Count said when he finished writing, "is to get in touch with a Priest who is a friend of mine and I know will make no difficulty in giving you your Marriage Certificate."

"I will pay whatever is necessary," the Viscount said.

"He will not charge," the Count replied, "but a small expression of gratitude for his Church will, I am sure, delight him."

"We are very grateful for his help and yours," the Viscount said.

"Now I will leave you," the Count announced. "I am only hoping your lovely wife will not find us at Dinner a collection of old bores."

"I am looking forward to a very enjoyable and exciting evening," the Princess said.

The Count smiled at her and left the room.

The Princess waited a moment as if to make sure he was out of hearing before she said:

"What is all this about?"

"Apparently due, as usual, to the Russians," the Viscount replied, "we have to explain at the frontier why we are going to Vienna, show that we are legally married, and that you are not just another Russian Spy."

The Princess threw up her hands.

"Can you imagine anything more tiresome? Do you really think he can get us a Marriage Certificate?"

"He says he can," the Viscount answered, "and I am sure he will not let us down."

The Princess gave a little shiver.

"I want to leave Hungary," she said. "I keep thinking of those two ghastly Russians watching the train steam out and asking themselves if they had been deceived."

"Why should you think they are doing that?" the Viscount enquired.

"The Russians sense things in a different way to other people," the Princess replied. "Although you may think I am being imaginative, I am sure they are sitting and thinking that somewhere, in some clever way, you have tricked them."

"I do not believe a word of it," the Viscount said firmly. "We have left them miles away. They looked in the carriage and saw nothing. You are just making yourself upset and miserable for no reason."

"You think that because you are English," the Princess answered. "But I am half Russian and, however much I try to forget it, I can, like my Father, sense and feel things, which you and Mama would say was sheer nonsense."

The Viscount had heard Russians talk like this before, and he said:

"I understand what you are saying. At the same

time, I think you are exaggerating the capability, or the brains, if you like, of two extremely unpleasant members of the Third Section. Forget them! We have left them behind, and I predict they will not worry us again."

"I only hope you are right," the Princess said. "Quite frankly, I am still frightened."

She went out of the room as she spoke.

The Viscount told himself that if she felt like that, there was nothing he could do to prevent it.

It was certainly no use arguing about it.

He rang for Bates and started to change for Dinner.

When he was ready, looking very smart in his evening-clothes, he went into the Princess's bedroom.

She too was dressed, and the Maid had left her.

She was wearing a gown of blue chiffon which was the colour of the night sky.

It was ornamented with tiny *diamanté* which glittered like stars.

As if to accentuate that she was a married woman, she was wearing diamond earrings.

Besides the flowers, two diamond stars were arranged in her hair.

The Viscount stood looking at her.

Then he said:

"There will be plenty of men here tonight who will tell you how beautiful you are. I am glad to be the first."

"That is a very pretty speech," the Princess replied, "and you are not so bad yourself."

They both laughed.

"Let us go down and make an entrance," the Viscount said. "Enjoy the compliments you will receive as soon as you appear, because after that I am quite certain it will just be 'the Russians!' 'The Russians!' 'The Russians!' "

The Princess laughed again.

"You are betting on a certainty. I am aware that the Hungarians have nothing else to talk about."

They went down the stairs side by side.

As the Viscount predicted, after one look at her the Guests found it difficult to find enough adjectives to praise her beauty.

'They are not quite as eloquent,' the Viscount thought, 'as the Austrians and the Parisians will be.'

It was, however, a good effort!

The Princess was the only woman present, and there were ten men round the Dining-Room table.

With the exception of the Viscount, they were all elderly.

They tried at the beginning of Dinner to amuse the Princess.

It was only later that they forgot her presence.

Then they started to tell the Viscount their troubles and difficulties, all of which were caused by the Russians.

When Dinner was finished, the Viscount thought that it would be tactful for the Princess to leave the room.

The men would be able to talk more freely than they had already.

When he suggested it to the Count, he shook his head.

He then raised his voice and said to his Guests:

"I hope you will excuse me if I leave you for a few minutes, but our Guests of Honour—the Viscount and the Viscountess Bredon—have some papers to sign which they have to take with them tomorrow morning. It will not take long. I can only ask you gentlemen to pass the time by enjoying the wines which I leave at your disposal."

They laughed at this but rose to their feet as the Count escorted the Princess and the Viscount from the room.

"I have been told the Priest is here," he said when they were outside. "I am sorry to learn it is not my friend who I thought would oblige me at this hour of night, but an older man who I know quite well but who is also slightly deaf."

"It is very kind of him to turn up so late," the Viscount said politely.

He thought they were walking towards the Count's Study, where he had talked to him earlier in the evening.

Instead, they went further along the passage.

"I must explain to you," the Count said. "I have a small Chapel here in the house which my Mother used when she was too old to go to the Cathedral. It was consecrated by the Archbishop and it made the last years of her life very happy that the Priest could come here several times a week to give her the Sacrament."

He opened a door as he spoke.

The Viscount saw that a small room had been converted very cleverly into a Chapel.

There was an altar with a Cross above it and six candles which were lit.

Two very large ones were standing each side of it.

An elderly man wearing a surplice was waiting for them.

The Count hurried forward to shake his hand.

"It is very kind of you to come, Father," he said. "As I sent a message to tell you, these young people have lost their Marriage Certificate and you know what trouble that causes at the Frontier."

"Yes! Yes!" the Priest agreed. "I know!"

He then spoke in a low voice into the Count's ear so quickly that the Viscount did not understand what he said.

The Count turned back to explain:

"The Priest said—and he is rather a stickler for what is correct—that he must say some prayers before he gives you the Marriage Certificate."

"I understand," the Viscount said.

The Count looked at the Princess.

"He asked, My Lady, if you will give him your

Wedding-Ring so that he can bless it."

The Viscount had already learnt that the ring on her left hand was her Mother's.

She also wore a ring set with five large diamonds.

She took off both.

The Viscount put the diamond ring in his pocket and handed the Wedding-Ring to the Priest.

He asked them to stand in front of him.

The Count moved away to sit on one of the chairs that were arranged at the back of the Chapel.

The old Priest spoke very slowly in a deep voice.

As the Viscount expected, he began with a prayer.

He thought this was typical of the trouble that the Russians managed to make wherever they went.

That they were using Russian women as Spies was nothing new.

Yet the War Office in England would make a note of it.

They would also be interested in the Officers who were starting Gymnasium Schools and finding other ways of stirring up trouble in the Balkans.

His thoughts were on the report he would write, when he heard his own name.

The Priest was saying:

"Lyle Nicholas Henry . . ."

He followed it with some words which the Viscount did not, for the moment, recognise.

Then quite suddenly it struck him that that was part of the Marriage Service and the Priest was speaking in Magyar.

He was now quite obviously asking him if he "took this woman to be his wife."

It flashed through the Viscount's mind that he must stop the Service.

Then he knew that was impossible.

For one thing, he had to have the Marriage Certificate.

For another, he could hardly confess, at this partic-

91

ular moment, that he and the Princess were not married.

What was more, if he was married, as he professed to be, why should it trouble him to repeat the Service?

It was only to placate the Priest, and give him a Certificate.

Almost inaudibly he heard himself say:

"I do!" in Hungarian.

Then the same question was put to the Princess.

She did not understand what was happening, but she had heard what the Viscount had said.

She simply repeated his words.

It was then that the old Priest blessed the ring and the Viscount placed it on the Princess's finger.

Then they knelt for the Blessing.

It did not take very long.

After they rose, they signed the Marriage Certificate.

The Viscount then thanked the Priest and gave him a large gratuity for his Church.

He was thinking that this never should have happened.

He was also wondering desperately how he could get out of it!

He did not wish to be married.

He was quite sure that the Princess did not wish to marry him!

By the time they had walked back to the Dining-Room, he was telling himself he had found a solution. Such an odd marriage could be dissolved if it was not consummated!

Vaguely at the back of his mind he remembered there was something in the Law which said that if one was forced into a marriage, it was illegal.

Alternatively, they could tear up the Marriage Certificate which no-one would have seen except the Count.

They could then forget that the Service had ever taken place.

All the same, he felt apprehensive.

He also felt somewhat guilty that he had not made it clear when they reached the Chapel that he just wanted the Certificate without anything else attached to it.

He could in a way understand that the Priest wished to be completely legal.

If he gave them the Certificate, there must be some evidence that the Marriage Service had taken place.

They were greeted back at the Dining-Room with enthusiasm.

After the Viscount had drunk a large Brandy, he began to feel less worried.

"I have got into this mess," he told himself, "and I must have enough brains to get myself out."

Finally the Guests left, delighted with their evening and what they had been able to tell him.

He, however, was worrying again.

To be honest, he had hardly heard some of the stories because he was thinking of himself and the Princess.

Yet he must have said the right thing, and given them hope, because they were all so cheerful when they said "good-night."

The Princess had slipped up to bed some time before the last man left.

She had said she was tired.

The Viscount thought she had every reason to be so after such a long day in the train.

There was also the fright of seeing those two particularly unpleasant members of the Third Section again.

He told himself sharply, the sooner they were on their way the better.

Bates helped him undress.

The Viscount gave him strict instructions that they must leave in plenty of time tomorrow morning.

"Just in case," he said, "there is any trouble when we cross the Frontier."

"Let's hope, M'Lord, there aren't too many Ruskies standing about there," Bates said. "We've had enough of them, we have."

"I agree with you," the Viscount answered. "So far we have been very lucky, but we must guard the Princess carefully. Having come so far, she cannot now be taken back to St. Petersburg."

"Not if I can 'elp it, M'Lord," Bates said. "Better dead, in my opinion, than living wi' that lot!"

The Viscount agreed, but he did not say so.

He merely waited until Bates had left him before he went into the Princess's room.

He had not made up his mind if he would tell her the truth so that they could try to find a solution together.

Perhaps it would be best to leave things as they were.

"She will have to know sooner or later," he told himself.

It would undoubtedly be a shock to find herself married when she least expected it.

He could not help thinking a little mockingly that any other young woman would be delighted to find herself married to him.

After all, he had so much to offer apart from himself.

Then he thought how the Princess's attitude had been entirely different to any other woman he had ever known.

'She is not the least in love with me,' he thought. 'Yet, having Russian blood, she should inevitably be very romantic.'

He knew the Russians quite well, enough to know that they were not all as brutal as the Tsar, who, anyway, was a German.

The real Russians loved, he had been told, not only with their hearts but with their souls.

To a Russian, love was something that was spiritual and affected them deeply.

The one blessing out of all this, whatever it might be, was that the Princess was not in love.

He thought it would have been far more difficult if she had loved him.

He had made it clear that he did not want her as his wife.

As he reached the communicating-door between their rooms, he hesitated a moment.

He was still asking the question if he should tell her or not.

Very quietly he pulled the door open.

Candles were still burning beside the large bed in which she seemed so small that for the moment he could hardly see her.

Then, as he approached nearer, he realised she was asleep.

She had obviously waited for him to come to say "good-night" and therefore had not blown out the candles.

She was fast asleep with her hair spread out over the pillow.

Her eye-lashes were very dark against her white skin.

She was completely relaxed.

There was just a faint smile on her perfectly formed lips, as if she were dreaming of something very pleasant.

The Viscount thought it would be impossible for anyone to paint a picture of a more beautiful woman asleep.

He stood looking at her for quite a long time.

He was wondering what would happen to her in the future.

When she reached England, would she find it as wonderful as she expected it to be?

He thought it was extremely touching that she was brave enough to have set off on her own.

Who else would have dared to elude the Tsar and refuse to obey his commands?

He could think of a large number of terrible things that might have happened to her.

He himself, if he had been a different sort of man, could have treated her very differently.

Then he remembered his Mother telling him that "Angels look after children."

Undoubtedly the Princess's Guardian Angel had been very busy as far as she was concerned.

At the same time, she had what the English called "guts," and that was lacking in a great number of people.

He had a sudden impulse to wake her up to tell her that he would get her to England if it was the last thing he ever did in his life.

Then he told himself he was being over-dramatic.

She expected him to do that anyway.

She trusted him and she had forced him to behave as what she called an "English Gentleman."

The Viscount took one last look at her.

Then he bent forward and blew out the candles one by one.

There was just enough moonlight coming through the window to guide him back to the communicating door.

As he went through it, he thought in some way it had been a strange experience.

He had been alone in a bedroom with a very beautiful woman but had not woken her.

Then he told himself he was thinking like a Russian!

He was smiling as he got into bed.

chapter five

THE Count saw them off at the Station with flowers for the Princess and a hamper of food for them to eat on the journey.

It would not take so long as it had coming from Lemburg to Budapest.

But they did not know if they would be delayed at the Frontier.

The Count was sad that they had to leave so quickly.

The Viscount promised that if it was possible, they would come back another time.

However, as the train steamed away from the Station, he said to the Princess:

"I have had quite enough of Hungary."

"I am so glad we are going away," she replied. "I have been frightened in case those awful men from the Third Section would catch up with us."

"Forget them!" the Viscount said. "We are now going to meet the happy and delightful Viennese, and I can assure you that they are very different."

The Count had arranged that they were locked in their carriage by the Guard, so that they would be alone.

Bates was next door.

As they had their food with them, it would be unnecessary for anyone to disturb them, except, of course, the Officials at the Frontier.

The train began to go more swiftly, and they were soon away from the houses and Castles of Budapest.

Unexpectedly, the Princess asked:

"What was all that fuss last night about our Marriage Certificate? I could not understand what the old man was saying in the Chapel, but I thought it would be a mistake for me to say so."

"He was speaking in Magyar," the Viscount replied, "which is the ancient language of Hungary and very difficult for most people to understand."

"I gathered it was something like that," the Princess said, "but I thought you would come to say 'good-night' to me when you came to bed, and I could ask you about it then."

"I did come," the Viscount replied, "but you were fast asleep."

"Then you must have been very late," the Princess said. "I waited and waited!"

"I am sorry about that," the Viscount answered, "but, as you can imagine, the Count had a great deal he wanted me to hear, and his friends had even more!"

The Princess laughed.

"They do make up a very sad story for themselves. At the same time, I am most sympathetic."

"So am I," the Viscount agreed.

She did not refer any more to the Marriage Service.

As they journeyed on, the Viscount decided it would be a mistake to upset her.

He found himself turning over and over in his mind how it was possible to get a marriage annulled.

The only thing he could do was to see a really good Lawyer as soon as they returned to England.

What was important was that there should be no publicity about it because that would reveal that the Princess had run away from St. Petersburg and that her Father had been a Russian.

He had been thinking that the best thing possible for her was to go back to her family.

Then there would be no gossip as to where she had come from, or that her Father had been a Russian.

Like most Aristocrats, the Duke of Wilthorpe resented having anything mentioned in the newspapers about his family.

The Viscount was sure that he could pass off the Princess's appearance without it attracting much notice.

"I shall say nothing," he told himself as the train passed through the wooded land which ended in the Frontier with Austria.

The train came to a standstill.

The Officials came on board to inspect the tickets, passports, and documents of all the travellers.

When the Guard unlocked the door of their carriage, the Viscount stepped onto the platform to exercise his legs.

The Princess, still nervous because they had not yet left Hungary, remained in the carriage.

The Viscount kept an eye on the Officials.

When they reached the front of the train where she was, he was waiting for them.

He produced his tickets, his passport, and the Marriage Certificate over which there had been so much trouble.

The Official glanced at it.

It seemed as if he were going to hand it back to the Viscount, when he gave an exclamation.

"What is it?" the Viscount asked.

"I see," he said, "that you are a Honeymoon couple and were married only last night."

"That is right," the Viscount agreed.

"Then, *Mein Herr*, you happen," the Official said, "to be our two hundredth Honeymoon couple this month."

He clapped his hands.

The young woman who had been waiting at the

end of the platform came running up with a bouquet of flowers.

"This is for your wife," the Official said, "and we welcome you to Vienna, where a special Ceremony awaits you."

The Viscount drew in his breath.

"That is very kind," he said, "but we are staying for only a very short time."

"The Ceremony will take place tonight, *Mein Herr*," the Official said, "and if you and your wife will come to the place written on this card, you will be given a free Dinner and a special welcome from a great number of other Honeymooning couples who are in Vienna at the moment."

The Princess thanked the girl for the flowers, and the Official then said:

"If you, *Mein Herr*, will let your wife stand on the platform, we have a photographer who has one of the new cameras to take a photograph of you."

The Viscount wanted to refuse.

But he could not think of a good reason why he should not want to be photographed.

He could only hope that as the cameras he had seen so far were new and not very accurate, when the picture appeared it would not be particularly recognisable.

The Princess was asked to stand beside him.

The photograph was taken after a great deal of arranging and the setting up of the camera on its stand.

Having taken them alone, the Official insisted that he and the other Officials who had been scrutinising the tickets should be included.

The girl who had brought the flowers was told to sit at their feet.

It all annoyed the Viscount.

It also made him apprehensive and afraid that it might somehow reach the newspapers.

At the same time, he could not think of any reason why he should refuse to do what they asked.

When the Princess got back into the train, the Official said:

"Now, do not forget, *Mein Herr*, we shall be waiting for you this evening and shall expect you to be with us at about seven o'clock."

"That is very kind of you," the Viscount replied. "My wife and I will do our best."

As the train moved into Austria, he could only think that it was a blessing that the Official had not realised he had a title.

It was not included on the Marriage Certificate, but it was definitely on his passport.

A Viscount was, however, an English title, and therefore the Official, not understanding it, addressed him as if he were an ordinary man.

"We do not have to go to their Dinner-Party, do we?" the Princess asked.

"No! Of course not!" the Viscount replied. "I will ask our Host, whoever it is, if we can notify them that we are regrettably unable to be present. I was just thinking that they did not notice my title and therefore we shall not be of any particular interest except to the Honeymoon Couples Club, or whatever it is called."

The Princess laughed.

"I think it is a charming idea of theirs, and just what I should expect to happen in Vienna."

The Viscount was thinking that it might have been very much worse if they had not had the Marriage Certificate.

That, of course, would have produced another problem, which he would have had to solve.

They reached Vienna about four o'clock in the afternoon.

As the train came to a stop, the Viscount was wondering who would meet him.

Lord Granville had originally suggested he should stay at the British Embassy.

But the Viscount had a very different idea.

He had been to Vienna before.

He had a great friend, Prince Anton Falkenberg, who had been at Oxford with him.

The Prince had stayed with him in England, and when he had visited him in Vienna had given him a most enjoyable time.

There had been visits to the Opera and a number of Balls.

It had also included the companionship of some very pretty and charming women.

If the Viscount had a reputation in London of being an ardent lover, Prince Anton surpassed him as "Don Juan" in Vienna.

They laughed about it together.

When the Prince had come to London, the Viscount had taken him to meet not only the Beauties who frequented Marlborough House.

He had also met the women who were acclaimed by those who visited the Music Halls, and the Ballet at Covent Garden.

He had given the Prince some riotous evenings at Romano's Supper Club.

He was sure that if the Prince was in Vienna, he would be thinking of how he could amuse him even better this time.

'Anton will certainly have a shock when I tell him I am married,' the Viscount thought.

The train came to a standstill.

He knew he would soon know whether he was to stay at the British Embassy or with the Prince.

The Servants from one place or the other would be waiting for him on the platform.

Their carriage was unlocked.

The Viscount saw a man hurrying towards him, but he was not able to determine immediately to whom he belonged.

Then a moment later the man was shaking him by the hand, saying:

"Welcome to Vienna, My Lord. His Highness was

sorry that he could not meet you himself, but he sent me to make his apologies and to convey you as swiftly as possible to his house, where he will be waiting for you."

The Viscount knew that after that everything would go smoothly.

The man who had met him was Prince Anton's Secretary, who behaved rather like an *Aide-de-Camp*.

With him were two Servants in very smart Livery to help Bates with the luggage.

The Secretary looked somewhat surprised when he realised there was a woman with the Viscount.

He hurriedly took them through the crowds to the front of the Station, where the Prince's carriage was waiting.

There was also another carriage for Bates and the luggage.

The Viscount did not explain to the Secretary who the Princess was.

They drove through the streets, in which were a great number of holiday-makers.

The Viscount had always thought that Vienna was one of the most beautiful cities he had ever visited.

He loved the warmth of its people, and the fact that they always seemed to be smiling.

It was such a contrast to the gloom of St. Petersburg and the apprehension of Hungary.

He felt himself relaxing in the sunshine.

The fountains were spraying their water up towards the sky.

As they passed over the Danube, it looked mysterious but at the same time romantic.

He knew the Princess was appreciating it in the same way as he was.

When they passed by the Stephanskirche she gave a little cry of delight.

"There is the Stephanskirche," she said. "I have seen pictures of it and I have wanted so much to visit it."

"We can do that tomorrow," the Viscount said.

"You will not forget?"

"I promise you I will not!"

He knew without her telling him that she wanted to say a prayer of thankfulness that they had escaped from Russia.

He thought it was typical of her that her prayers meant so much.

Unlike so many other women, she was grateful for what was given her, especially when it came from God.

The Prince's house, which the Viscount knew well, was on the outskirts of Vienna.

It had been built by one of his ancestors right on the Danube.

In fact, one wall of what was more of a Castle than a house literally rose above the river itself.

There were balconies outside a number of the windows.

In the front there was a garden filled at the moment with spring flowers and shrubs in blossom.

There was also a very impressive entrance where, as the carriage drove up the drive, the Viscount saw his friend waiting.

As the horses came to a standstill, the Prince, who was a tall, slim man, threw out his arms in a gesture of welcome.

"Lyle! Lyle!" he exclaimed. "It is wonderful to see you! It is far too long since you have paid me a visit."

"I might say the same, Anton!" the Viscount replied as he got out of the carriage. "London is waiting for you."

The Prince laughed.

He was not exactly handsome, but he had a very attractive face and eyes which always seemed to be twinkling with laughter.

Now, when he looked curiously at the Princess, the Viscount said:

"Let me introduce my wife?"

The Prince gave an audible gasp.

"Your wife?" he exclaimed. "Why did you not tell me you had been married?"

"It is a long story which I will tell you later," the Viscount replied.

The Prince was bowing over the Princess's hand.

"I might have known," he said, "that if Lyle did marry, he would find the most beautiful woman in the world to become his wife."

The Princess smiled, and the dimples appeared on either side of her mouth.

"I hope you do not mind me coming here with my husband," she said, "when you had not been warned that I was with him."

"Now that I have seen you," the Prince answered, "I should have been desolate if he had left you behind."

He went into the house which, as the Viscount had said before, was really a Palace.

But the Prince's country residence to which the name belonged was still occupied by his Father.

The house in Vienna had been given to him for his own use.

The rooms were large and beautifully decorated.

The Prince had a great many Servants waiting on him.

He took the Viscount and the Princess into his Drawing-Room.

Two servants hurried round with drinks and delicious sweetmeats for them to eat.

"What sort of journey did you have?" the Prince asked.

"I will tell you later," the Viscount answered. "But for the moment I want to hear what you have been doing and why you have not communicated with me for such a long time."

The Prince was quick-witted enough to realise that there was some secret.

It was obviously something the Viscount would divulge to him when they were alone.

He therefore went into a long explanation of how he had been travelling in many parts of the world.

That was the reason he had not been to England.

"Anyway, as you well know, Lyle, I am a rotten letter writer," he ended. "Although I admit I might have sent you a postcard or two."

The Viscount thought the Princess would want to take off her hat.

She might also want to rest after the journey.

She was taken upstairs, where she found a House-keeper and a Maid to attend her.

When they were alone, the Prince turned to the Viscount and said:

"Now, what is going on, Lyle? How did you find anyone so exquisitely beautiful?"

The Viscount hesitated for a moment, and then he said:

"Because you are my oldest friend and because I trust you, I will tell you the truth of what has happened. Quite frankly, I need your advice."

The Prince poured him out another glass of wine and said:

"Talk away, I am listening!"

The Viscount began by telling him what had happened on the train from St. Petersburg.

He finished by explaining how, after escaping from the Third Section to get into Austria, he had been trapped into Matrimony.

The Prince could only gasp.

"All this could happen only to you, Lyle," he said. "I cannot believe I am not listening to some Fairy-Story out of the *Arabian Nights*."

"Unfortunately, it is all true," the Viscount said, "and now I am not certain whether it would be possible to have the marriage annulled."

"Annulled! Why on earth do you want it annulled?" the Prince enquired. "You have to marry some time, as you well know, to have an heir. You could not have found anyone more exquisite, more beautiful to be your wife."

"You know as well as I do," the Viscount replied, "that we have always said we would not settle down until it was absolutely obligatory!"

"That is true," the Prince agreed. "But I can tell you quite truthfully that in all my various love affairs, I have never been fortunate to find anyone quite so lovely as your wife. In fact, I think it is a pity I did not meet her first."

"Now, do behave yourself, Anton," the Viscount said. "As I have just told you, I am in a hell of a fix. Yentha does not love me and I do not love her. It is a mistake, as you and I have often said, to have an arranged marriage."

It was true that they had talked in the past of the marriages that were arranged in England, not only among Royalty but also among the distinguished families.

As the Prince knew, on the Continent the ancient families of France, Austria, and Italy always chose for their sons and daughters a Bride or a Bridegroom of equal Social importance.

If they wanted love, it was something which happened outside marriage, whilst inside, the conventions were observed.

"I expect you will find a solution one way or another," the Prince was saying now. "As the Princess is your wife, I shall have to change the programme I have arranged for you while you are with me."

"I thought that would be inevitable," the Viscount said rather bitterly. "What am I missing?"

"There would be no point in telling you that," the Prince said. "I shall just have to cancel one or two engagements and make sure those I am entertaining here are more or less respectable."

The Viscount knew that this meant the Prince would have to cancel the women who had been invited for Dinner.

It was very unlikely that later in the evening he and the Prince would "do the town" as they had done in the past.

He walked towards the window to look out at the Danube moving slowly by.

"I have got myself into a mess, Anton," he said. "I cannot quite see how I could have avoided it without refusing to help Yentha in the first place."

"Well, naturally, you could not hand the girl over to those devils," the Prince agreed. "We have had enough of them causing trouble here, which I will not bore you with, as I know you have heard it all already."

"That is true enough," the Viscount replied. "In fact, I have heard so much that if I ever see a Russian again, I shall feel like shooting him."

"A good thing, too," the Prince said. "But we have managed at the moment, more or less, to keep some control over them, in Vienna at any rate."

He then threw out his arms.

"Let us forget them," he said. "You are here, and I want you to enjoy yourself. What we will do tonight is quite different to what I intended. But I still think it will be fun!"

Because his enthusiasm was infectious, the Viscount thought that was true.

As the Prince sent for his Secretary to make a great many alterations to what had been planned, he sat down to listen.

What eventually was planned was that the Ladies of the Dinner-Party would be changed.

As the Prince gave him a short cameo of each woman he discarded, the Viscount thought he was missing something rather unique.

He would have enjoyed them enormously if he had been alone.

Their places were taken by Ladies of the Social World.

The Prince assured him they were beautiful, amusing, and also intelligent.

"Perhaps it is a blessing in disguise," he said to cheer up the Viscount. "You know as well as I do, Lyle, the 'soiled Doves' of this world have nothing to say. They look pretty and their performance is unquestionable, but you do not have to use your brain to appreciate it."

"I cannot remember you worrying much about your brain when you were in London," the Viscount remarked.

The Prince laughed.

"There is a time for everything, and I must say that little Ballet Dancer you produced for me was adorable. I have often thought of her. What is she doing now?"

"When I last heard of her," the Viscount replied, "she relied for her protection on a very rich but, in my opinion, a very boring old man."

The Prince laughed.

"A sad story. I must turn up one day and try to cheer her up."

He then told the Viscount that when Dinner was over, they would all proceed to a Party.

It was taking place just a very short distance from his house.

"I originally refused," he said, "because I had other plans for you and I together. But as Johann Strauss is providing the music, I am quite certain it is something your wife would enjoy."

"I am sure she would," the Viscount replied.

He could not help thinking he would enjoy it if he had been alone with the Prince, as had been planned originally.

'Women and Russians,' he thought to himself. 'They always muck everything up!'

When he went upstairs he found that Yentha had been given the bedroom that he himself usually slept in when he came to Vienna.

He liked it particularly because it had a huge bow window opening onto one of the balconies which hung out over the Danube.

It had fascinated him on his very first visit.

He looked down at the river moving slowly past and thought how long and strong it was.

How it passed through so many countries before it finally reached the sea.

There was, he thought, something very romantic about the Danube.

He had not been surprised when he had heard in England that Johann Strauss had written a dance tune called "The Blue Danube."

Now it irritated him a little to think that Yentha would sleep in the bed he had occupied.

He would have to sleep in the Dressing-Room.

He had not accentuated this to the Prince.

He thought he had understood that if he had had any chance of dissolving the marriage, it must certainly not be consummated.

Yentha smiled at him when he came into the bedroom.

The Maids who were with her tactfully withdrew.

She was lying on the bed.

The bath that she was to take before Dinner was arranged in front of the mantelpiece.

The hot and cold water for it had not yet been brought upstairs.

"What are we doing tonight?" Yentha asked as he walked towards her.

"You are to put on your best 'bib and tucker,' " the Viscount replied, "because we are having a very Social evening."

She laughed.

"I am not so stupid," she said, "as not to realise that you and the Prince expected to go off on your own! Because I have appeared, everything has been spoilt."

"Not exactly spoilt," the Viscount said tactfully,

"but somewhat changed. Now you have got a chance, if you want, to wear your tiara."

"As grand as that?" Yentha enquired. "Remember it is my Mother's and very impressive."

"Then impress them," the Viscount said. "If I have to have a wife, I am delighted that like my friend the Prince, they should envy me."

When he finished speaking, he thought he had been rather rude.

As he looked at Yentha apologetically, she said:

"I know you are angry because we were properly married last night, were we not?"

The Viscount nodded.

"I did not realise it at first," he said, "because the Priest was speaking in Magyar. Then I could not see what I could do about it."

"If you had stopped him, I doubt if he would have given you the Marriage Certificate," Yentha said. "He was obviously a very Holy Man who would not tell a lie."

"I am sure when we get to London we can do something about it," the Viscount said, "and we shall be there in a few days' time."

"We are not going to stay here?" Yentha asked.

The Viscount shook his head.

"I am due in Paris and perhaps, if I had been alone, I would have played truant for the next day or two. But considering what you have told me and what I have learnt on the journey, the sooner I get back to England the better."

"I understand," Yentha said, "and of course that will mean the . . . sooner you . . . will get . . . rid of . . . me."

"You are making me sound very brutal and very unsympathetic," the Viscount complained. "It is just unfortunate that what happened last night should make things very much more difficult than they would have been otherwise."

"I am . . . sorry!" she said softly. "It is all my . . .

fault for thrusting . . . myself upon you. I shall never be able to . . . thank you . . . enough for . . . helping me when I most . . . needed help."

The Viscount saw a little shiver run through her.

He knew that she was thinking that if he had refused to help her, she would undoubtedly have been taken back to St. Petersburg and forced to do what the Tsar wished.

The Viscount suddenly felt ashamed of himself.

He sat down on the side of the bed and took Yentha's hand in his.

"Now, listen!" he said. "This is all an adventure, and the best thing both of us can do is to enjoy it as much as we can."

He looked at her searchingly before he went on:

"Tonight I want you to shine like a rising star so that everyone will think I am the cleverest man in the world to have found you. Tomorrow, when it comes, we will face what new problems confront us, if there are any."

Yentha's fingers closed over his.

"It is very . . . exciting for . . . me to be with . . . you," she said, "and perhaps one day I shall be . . . able to . . . thank you."

The Viscount raised her hand to his lips.

Then he said:

"Get dressed! Do not forget how I am expecting you to look!"

He walked across the room, stopping for a moment at the bow window.

It was very warm.

He thought how much he had enjoyed leaning over the balcony, feeling the sun on his head as he watched it shimmering on the moving water beneath him.

Then he opened the communicating door and went into the room, where Bates was waiting for him.

"It's nice to be back, M'Lord!" the Valet said cheerfully.

"That is just what I was thinking," the Viscount replied.

At the same time, he resented that his room did not have a balcony.

Also that the bed was very much smaller than the one in which Yentha would sleep alone.

He had his bath and changed into his evening-clothes.

He thought it was rather a pity that he could not wear his decorations.

It would certainly not have been necessary if the original Party that the Prince had planned had taken place.

But now, as there was to be no Royalty present with the exception of the Host, the glitter must be left to the Ladies.

When he was ready, he knocked on the communicating door.

He found Yentha waiting for him.

One look at her told him that she was everything he had hoped and expected but a million times better.

She had on the diamond tiara which had belonged to her Mother.

It was large and very impressive.

On her dark hair it made her look very tall, very distinguished, and, the Viscount had to admit, Royal.

There were diamonds round her neck, in her ears, and on her wrists.

Her dress seemed to glisten and glitter with every movement she made.

"Do I look all right?" she asked, as he had not spoken.

"You look magnificent," he answered, "and they will doubtless all be as impressed as I want them to be."

There was a little twinge in his voice.

It told her he was thinking that if he had to be married, he might as well have a wife whom other women would envy and men would admire.

113

She gave a deep sigh to herself.

She was thinking in her desperation that she had never had any wish to upset anyone, least of all the man who had been so kind to her.

'I am sure something can be done when we get to England,' she thought consolingly.

Then, as the Viscount held out his arm, she slipped her hand into it.

They walked down the stairs side by side.

The Viscount had expected Yentha to be a success.

He had not, however, anticipated that every man who had come to Dinner would find it difficult to keep his eyes off her.

For the first time, the Viscount saw his wife taking the position to which she was entitled.

She was sitting on her Host's right.

There was no doubt that the Prince was not pretending to find her enchanting.

The Viscount knew him so well, he was aware Anton was, in fact, captivated by Yentha.

He was doing his very experienced best to flirt with her, almost outrageously.

He had a rival in the man on the other side.

He was, the Viscount knew, a very distinguished Viennese, and he struggled all the evening to capture Yentha's attention.

To the Viscount's surprise, she was not in the least overwhelmed by either of these two men, nor the rest, who also tried to ingratiate themselves.

She laughed at their compliments, which did not make her in the least shy.

She had plenty to talk about besides herself.

The Viscount's experience with the many sophisticated married women with whom he had had *affaires de coeur* was that the conversation invariably concerned themselves and love.

Listening, he knew that Yentha had a lot to say on other subjects.

She also managed, he noticed, in a somewhat subtle

way to make the men who wanted to talk about her talk about themselves.

On either side of him at Dinner the Prince had put two acknowledged Viennese Beauties, both of whom were past-masters in the art of discreet *affaires de coeur*.

For some reason he did not understand, the Viscount was not particularly interested in either of them.

He found himself watching the little tricks that every woman used when she was on the "war-path."

He decided they were somewhat banal.

His eyes kept straying across the table to where his wife was making two men laugh.

At the same time, she was making every woman at the table seem somewhat ordinary.

"She is certainly unique," he told himself.

When Dinner was finished, and it lasted quite a long time, they all went, as the Prince had arranged, to a Party.

It was being held in one of his friend's houses, only a short distance away.

As they entered the Ball-Room, Johann Strauss's romantic tunes filled the air.

Before anyone else could ask her, Yentha said to the Viscount:

"Please dance this with me. I have always dreamt that it was something I might do one day."

Regardless that it might seem rather rude to their Host and Hostess, who had not finished shaking hands with the Prince's party, the Viscount swung her on to the floor.

As he had somehow expected, she was as light as thistledown.

As they twirled round, he knew she was a perfect dancer.

Whatever he did, she followed him.

The band was conducted by Johann Strauss, who the Viscount knew quite well.

The son of his famous Father who became Musical

Director to the Court, he had exceptional charm, temperament, and inventiveness.

He was only nineteen when he had his own orchestra.

Five years later he took over his Father's and toured England and America with it.

He made the Viennese Waltz world-famous and was called the "Waltz King."

The Viscount and Yentha danced until the music came to an end.

"That was wonderful," she exclaimed. "Now one of my dreams has come true."

"Let us hope that there are many others which will do the same," the Viscount replied.

She saw the Prince was hurrying towards her.

"Please dance with me again," she said quickly, "before we have to go home."

"But of course!" the Viscount answered. "I claim the dance after this. I can see quite clearly what our host intends."

He found, not particularly to his surprise, that he had a great difficulty in dancing with his wife for the second time.

In fact, he had almost a quarrel with one man.

He persisted in saying it was his turn and he had no right to interfere.

"I think I have every right!" the Viscount replied.

He thought, although it was the truth, it was a strange thing for him to have to say.

It was obvious from the moment she arrived that Yentha was the success of the evening.

She seemed to stand out amongst the other women.

That she was enjoying herself seemed to vibrate from her so that everyone who was with her appeared happy too.

It was one o'clock, and the Viscount said when he approached her:

"I think, as we have been travelling all day, this

should be the last dance with me, and then I will take you home."

She moved quickly into his arms.

Two men protested loudly that she had promised to dance with them.

"Another time," she said as the Viscount swept her away.

"And when will that be?" one of them asked.

"When you come to England," she answered, and saw the disappointment on his face.

"You have been a great success," the Viscount said as they moved slowly to a romantic Waltz.

"I wanted you to be proud of me," she answered, "even though I am a nuisance."

"I have not said that you were," the Viscount replied.

"But you thought it," she said. "I saw it in your eyes and felt it in your vibrations coming out towards me."

"If that is the truth, I can only apologise."

She smiled at him.

"It is not so bad at the moment, so stop worrying. Tomorrow may never come."

"I hope that is not true!" the Viscount exclaimed.

"One never knows," she answered. "That is why I am enjoying every moment of this Waltz with you."

She thought it was a mistake to spoil it with conversation.

They danced in silence until just before the dance came to an end and the Viscount swept her out of the Ball-Room.

"Now I am taking you home," he said. "Otherwise you will be far too tired to travel tomorrow. I have decided that we must go on to Paris."

Yentha did not answer.

She merely took her cloak from the Servant who was holding it out for her.

They stepped into one of the carriages which was waiting outside.

The Prince had told them that if they wanted to leave, one of his carriages was always in attendance.

"Nothing is worse," he had said, "than to have to hang about waiting for other people."

The Viscount thought this was true.

As they drove back towards the Prince's house, he was grateful for the Prince's excellent organisation.

The Night-Footman let them in, and they went up the stairs.

The Viscount opened the door of Yentha's bedroom and saw the lights had been left on by the bed.

As the windows were open on to the balcony, the moonlight was also streaming in like a silver flood.

"Go to bed, Yentha," he said, "and dream you are still dancing. Can you manage to undo your dress, or shall I do it for you?"

She turned her back to him.

"Just the top," she said. "I told the Maids not to wait up. I thought we would be very late."

"That was considerate of you," he said. "I said the same to Bates."

He undid the buttons at the top of her gown, and she assured him she could manage everything else.

She had already taken off her tiara and put it down on the Dressing-Table.

"Good-night, Yentha!" the Viscount said. "You looked very lovely tonight, as you well know."

"I shall always remember that I have danced with you to Johann Strauss," she replied.

The Viscount went into his own room.

He opened the windows even wider than they were already.

It was undoubtedly a very hot night, without a breath of wind.

He saw with relief that Bates had left a cold bath ready for him.

When he was undressed he got into it, finding it both cool and refreshing.

He was, however, tired, and he did not linger very long.

He got out and started to dry himself.

As he did so, he stood in front of the window, thinking how beautiful the moonlight was and the sky filled with stars.

It was then he heard Yentha scream.

For a moment he thought he must have been mistaken. Then there was another scream.

Instinctively, tucking his towel round his waist, he turned towards the communicating door.

As he opened it, he heard the explosion of a pistol-shot.

chapter six

LOOKING across the room which was bright in the moonlight, the Viscount could see Yentha.

She was sitting up in bed with a pistol in her hand.

A man was on the end of the bed and obviously moving towards her.

As she shot him, he fell backwards.

With a swiftness of an athlete the Viscount rushed across the room.

He caught the man as he was falling and dragged him from the bed on to the floor.

He pulled him towards the window and onto the balcony.

As he did so, he was aware that the man who had been shot was one of the Russians who had come to his carriage at Lemburg.

The Viscount thought that the Russian was alive, but dazed by the shock.

Using all his strength, he hit the villain's forehead violently against the stone balustrade of the balcony.

Then he picked him up and threw him into the river below.

There was a loud splash.

The Viscount bent over to see the Russian rise in the water and then start to float downstream.

He was suddenly aware that directly below the balcony there was the other Russian in a small boat who was reaching out towards his companion's body.

When the Viscount dragged the Russian towards the window, he heard, when they reached the balcony, a slight tinkle as if he had dropped something.

When he looked down he saw a very sharp dagger shining in the moonlight.

He picked it up and bent over the balcony.

Now he could see the Russian he had thrown into the water was moving quickly.

Below in the boat the other Russian was trying desperately to catch hold of him as he passed.

The Viscount raised the dagger above his head.

Again using all of his very considerable strength, he threw it down at the man below.

With an accuracy which came through experience, the dagger pierced the Russian right in the centre of his back.

As he was leaning forward, the force of it toppled him into the river.

He fell face downwards.

As the moonlight glittered on the dagger, the Viscount knew that if he was not dead, he would undoubtedly be drowned.

He thought with satisfaction that that had disposed of both of them.

They were the two who the Princess had quite rightly been afraid would follow them to Vienna.

He turned back towards the window.

Now her fear of these Russians, at any rate, was at an end.

Then, as he entered the room, he saw she was sitting up, the way he had last seen her.

She was still holding the small jewelled revolver in her hand.

He went quickly towards her, and as he sat down on the bed, she said in a small, terrified voice:

"I . . . killed . . . him! I . . . killed . . . him!"

"You wounded him!" the Viscount said. "And now

he has drowned and will not trouble you again."

Then he realised that she had not actually heard him and was trembling all over.

"I . . . killed . . . him!" she whispered.

The Viscount put his arms round her.

"You have been very brave, and it was very clever of you," he said. "Now you need not worry about them any more."

Because she was shaking all over, he pulled her a little closer.

She looked up at him and whispered:

"It . . . is . . . wicked to . . . kill . . . anybody."

The Viscount could see the tears and the expression of shock in her eyes.

Because she looked so pathetic and at the same time so lovely, without really thinking about it he kissed her.

It was a very gentle kiss.

Then, as his lips met hers, he was aware that a streak of lightning shot through him.

It was something he had never felt before.

The pressure of his lips grew harder.

At the same time, he gently pushed her backwards on to the pillow.

Then, as he kissed her and went on kissing her, he thought he had never known anything so exciting.

Yet it was different to any kiss he had ever known.

He was aware that when his lips first touched hers, Yentha had stiffened.

But now he thought she was feeling as he did.

There was an ecstasy between them which made it impossible to think, only to feel.

It was then he was aware that, because it had been so hot, Yentha had gone to bed naked.

Her breasts were soft against his chest, and it was the most exquisite feeling he had ever known.

His kisses became more demanding, more passionate.

Yet it was not the same burning, fiery passion he had known before.

It was more subtle, more like the moonlight itself, but even more intense.

Then, as he felt Yentha's body melt into his, he was carrying her up into the sky.

They were part of the moonlight which enveloped them.

The stars were glittering on their lips and in their hearts.

A long time later the Viscount asked in a voice that was deep and unsteady:

"I have not frightened you, my Darling?"

Yentha moved her cheek against his chest.

"I . . . had no . . . idea," she whispered, "that . . . love was . . . so . . . wonderful."

"Is that what I made you feel?" the Viscount asked.

"It was the . . . most . . . marvellous . . . perfect thing that has ever . . . happened to . . . me," she murmured. "So . . . wonderful it is . . . difficult to . . . believe it . . . is true."

The Viscount tightened his arms round her.

"It was true," he said, "but I was afraid you would be frightened because you did not love me."

"I love . . . you! Of course . . . I love . . . you!" Yentha answered. "But I . . . knew you . . . did not . . . love me."

"When did you first know you loved me?" the Viscount asked.

He felt her move a little closer to him.

"I think," she said, "I really . . . loved you . . . from the first . . . time I saw you, when you were . . . so kind . . . to me and . . . did not . . . send me away, as I was . . . afraid you . . . might do."

She drew in her breath before she said:

"But I did not . . . realise it was . . . love. I just thought how . . . wonderful you . . . were and . . . then

124

I was . . . afraid . . . desperately . . . afraid of . . . losing you."

The Viscount remembered that was what he had intended to do. Aloud he asked:

"Then what happened?"

"I think I . . . realised I was . . . in love . . . with you . . . when you were so . . . clever and . . . lifted me up . . . into the luggage-rack. I told . . . you afterwards . . . that . . . those men would . . . follow us."

Just for a moment there was a faint echo of fear in her voice.

"It is something they will never do again," the Viscount said.

"You are quite . . . sure they . . . are both . . . dead? But perhaps it was . . . wrong and . . . wicked of . . . me to . . . kill anybody."

The Viscount moved his lips against the softness of her forehead.

"I think you wounded him," he said, "but I made certain he was unconscious when I threw him into the river. He would therefore drown."

"I . . . I . . . it was very . . . frightening to . . . see him . . . there on my . . . bed," Yentha murmured.

"I know it must have been," the Viscount said gently, "and of course it was all due to us being the two hundredth Honeymoon couple at the Frontier! When the Russians followed us and asked if they could remember me, the Officials would have told them that you were with me."

The Princess put up her hand to hold on to him.

It was as if she were afraid that even now she might be taken from him.

"We might have guessed that getting the Marriage Certificate," the Viscount said, "would eventually lead to us being married one way or another!"

There was a touch of amusement in his voice.

"I thought that it would make you very angry," the Princess said in a small voice.

The Viscount thought of how he had believed the

marriage might be annulled.

He knew now it was something he did not want and would never allow.

"We are married!" he said almost fiercely. "Now you are mine and I will never lose you. Never!"

"That is . . . what I . . . wanted you to . . . say," Yentha answered. "But do you . . . really . . . love . . . me?"

"I love you as I have never loved any woman before," the Viscount said, "and like you, because it was so strange, I did not recognise it as love. I believe now we were made for each other."

"That is what I have . . . felt ever . . . since I . . . loved you," Yentha said. "We have . . . found each . . . other again and now we can . . . be together."

"I shall make sure of that," the Viscount said, "and, my Darling, Precious little wife, you are everything I ever wanted to find, but thought it was impossible."

"You . . . are quite, quite . . . sure that is . . . true?" she asked. "When I realised what the Priest was . . . doing I was very . . . frightened that you . . . would stop . . . the marriage."

"That was something I could not do," the Viscount replied. "Now I realise that your Guardian Angel, or perhaps your Father and Mother, made quite certain that we should escape from Hungary and that you would be with me for the rest of your life."

"That . . . is what I . . . want," Yentha said. "I want to be with . . . you and even . . . now I am . . . after you have . . . taken me up into . . . Paradise . . . afraid of . . . losing you."

"That is exactly what happened," the Viscount said. "It was also, my Precious, Paradise for me!"

"You are quite . . . sure of that?" Yentha asked. "After all . . . as I tried to . . . explain to you . . . being half Russian, I love . . . you not only . . . with my heart . . . but with my . . . soul. It was my soul . . . which felt that we . . . touched the . . . stars."

"That is what I felt," the Viscount said, "and as I have already told you, no-one has ever given me such

126

ecstasy. I have never before touched the peaks of a love that is completely and utterly different to anything I have ever known."

Yentha gave a little cry of happiness.

Her arm went round the Viscount's neck, pulling his head down to hers.

Then he was kissing her again wildly, passionately, possessively, as if he were afraid of losing her.

It was fairly late the following morning when the Viscount went downstairs to find the Prince.

He was in his Study.

When the Viscount went in, he said:

"I have made all the arrangements, Lyle, that you have asked for. I wish you could stay longer."

"I wish I could, too," the Viscount replied, "but I have to obey my orders and go to Paris, and then I can go home."

The Prince looked at him and said:

"You look somehow different today, and very pleased with yourself. What has happened?"

"I am, Anton," the Viscount replied, "really in love for the first time in my life, and I find it a very magical experience."

The Prince threw up his hands.

"You are in love! That is what I wanted you to be, and I know that that enchanting young woman is exactly the wife I should have chosen for you."

"Then you must come to see us when we are settled in England," the Viscount replied.

"It is something I have every intention of doing," the Prince answered, "and I will be Godfather to your first son."

While they were talking, the Viscount was turning over in his mind whether he should tell the Prince what had happened last night.

Then he thought it would be best to say nothing.

After all, when the dead men were found, they would be a long way away from the Prince's house.

There was no reason why anyone should connect them with him.

Because the house was so large, no-one had heard the shot from Yentha's small pistol.

There would be nothing to make anyone suspect that the Russian had climbed up into her bedroom from the river.

He had looked out early that morning to see that the boat was no longer there.

It had followed the dead Russians down the river on the current.

It was a case, the Viscount told himself, of "letting sleeping dogs lie."

"I think, Anton," he said aloud, "it was the magic of you, Vienna, and, of course, Johann Strauss which brought Yentha's and my love to the surface, and we are both ecstatically happy."

"How could you possibly resist such a combination?" the Prince asked. "Of course, as your oldest and closest friend, I cannot tell you how happy I am."

He said very much the same thing to Yentha.

For the first time since he had known her, the Viscount saw her blush and look a little shy.

He knew it was because she was vividly conscious of her love for him.

Her eyes were very expressive.

The Prince saw them off on the mid-day train which left for Paris and in which they had to spend the night.

He had made all the arrangements.

They had the most comfortable carriage with a Drawing-Room, two bedrooms, and there was actually a corridor.

These had only just been introduced in Europe.

The Viscount had to admit it was very much more convenient than the old method of having to get in and out at every stop.

The Prince had filled what was their Drawing-Room with flowers.

There was not only food for the journey, but also some bottles of Champagne.

"You are more than kind," the Viscount said.

"Do not forget you are still on your Honeymoon," the Prince replied. "Though I would very much like to come with you, I am quite certain I should be very much *de trop.*"

He laughed at that and he kissed the Bride "good-bye."

"You are so beautiful," he said. "I only wish I had found you first, but then, Lyle has always beaten me at games, and I have therefore to put up with him taking the most beautiful woman in the world away from me."

The Princess laughed a little shyly.

When the train had left the Station and they had waved until the Prince was out of sight, she said:

"He is so kind. I am not surprised he was your closest friend."

"Because we have meant so much to each other," the Viscount said, "I am glad that you and I found each other when we were in his house."

"You did not tell him about the Russians?" Yentha enquired.

The Viscount shook his head.

"What was the point? It might worry him, and if there are any questions asked, he will genuinely not know the answers."

"I feel quite different now they are no longer after us," Yentha said. "I know you do not believe that a Russian has second sight, or uses his Third Eye or any of those things, but I promise you, the world seems to me as if the last menace has gone and I no longer need be afraid."

It just flashed through the Viscount's mind that perhaps the Tsar would still be waiting to hear what had happened to Yentha.

Alexander might want to know how she had escaped from him.

The Viscount knew, however, it was something he must not put into words.

It could spoil the happiness that he could feel vibrating from her towards him.

Instead, he just put his arms round her and kissed her.

Once again, because he was touching her, there was that strange ecstasy which made them both breathless.

Having been rather silent the day before, now they found they had a million things to say to each other.

For the first time, the Viscount wanted to hear about Yentha's childhood.

He wished to know which members of her family she had communicated with since her Mother's death.

Also, whom she had expected to meet when they reached England.

It was rather a relief, he thought, to find that she had in fact been almost ignored by the family.

The Duke had been furious when his daughter had married a Russian and gone to live in Russia.

While the Princess's Mother had written to her Mother before she died, her Father had always remained very much aloof.

"Grandpapa loathed the Russians for no particular reason," Yentha said, "and I think if you try to avoid saying my Father was one, it will please him."

"It should certainly make things easier," the Viscount replied.

He was just wondering, although he did not say so to Yentha, if, when their marriage was announced, the news would somehow reach St. Petersburg.

He could not imagine, under the circumstances, that the Tsar would continue to send the Third Section after her, especially at a moment when there was the threat of another War with England.

Yet because Alexander was such an unpredictable man, he might do anything.

But the one thing the Viscount was determined upon was that his wife would not be upset.

Every moment he touched her he felt he loved her more.

He knew he must keep her from being worried or frightened.

Because they were together, the journey seemed to flash by on wings.

Although they slept together in one small bed, it seemed like a magic Palace and their happiness made it a bower of flowers.

"The only thing that worries me," Yentha said, "is that our wedding was so strange, it will be difficult to remember it as the most important day of my life, as I would like to do."

"Then I can quite easily remedy that," the Viscount replied.

"How?" she asked.

"We will be married again in England, although it will be called a Service of Blessing. My Father has a Chapel attached to his house and I am sure that your Grandfather has one at his."

"I never asked Mama that," Yentha said. "She told me how she and Papa ran away and were married in Russia in the little Church where nobody had any idea that Papa was a Prince."

"You seem, as a family, to be rather addicted to running away," the Viscount said, "and it is something, my Precious, you will never do from me."

"As though I want to!" Yentha answered. "I love . . . you! I love . . . you! I want to keep saying it over and over again in case . . . you do not . . . believe me."

"It is what I want to say to you," the Viscount replied. "I was just thinking that I love you more at this moment than I loved you three minutes ago."

She laughed.

"I wonder what the ultimate number will be, if it increases so rapidly."

"I will tell you when we get to it," the Viscount said.

He was touching her very gently as he spoke.

He felt the quiver that went through her.

He knew that every time he made love to her he increased the passionate little flames of love which echoed the burning fire within himself.

He had been aware from the beginning there was something so very spiritual about what they felt for each other.

It could not be compared with anything else he had ever known.

"How can you be so different?" he asked unexpectedly.

She looked up at him a little apprehensively.

"Different to what?" she asked.

"To other women I have known. I imagined, perhaps in my ignorance, that they loved me."

"Of course they must have loved you," Yentha replied. "How could they help it when you are so . . . handsome . . . so clever . . . and so very, very . . . wonderful."

"That is what I want you to think," he said. "At the same time, my Precious one, we have something between us that is different and which we must never lose."

"We will never do that," she answered. "Now again I am being Russian when I say the love I feel for you covers the whole world and I am nothing without it."

She shook her head and said:

"I am explaining it very badly, but there are no words."

"You will just have to feel what I am feeling," the Viscount said in a deep voice, "just as I know what you are thinking and you know that I love you."

"I adore you, and I worship you!" Yentha said. "You are everything a man should be."

The Viscount gave a little laugh.

"Am I at last the perfect English Gentleman you have been trying to make me?"

"You have always been that, and so much more,"

the Princess said. "You were a Gentleman because you helped me when I was in distress, but you are also the Knight in Shining Armour in that you saved me when I was threatened."

Her voice deepened as she added:

"And a God-like Archangel who ... carried me ... up to a ... Paradise ... amongst the ... stars."

The way she spoke was very moving.

Because there were no words to express what he felt, the Viscount could only kiss her.

Once again their love carried them up into the sky.

They arrived in Paris late in the evening and there were carriages waiting for them from the British Embassy.

As they drove through the streets bright with lights, Yentha said:

"This is almost as exciting as going to Vienna. I wish there were a Johann Strauss for us to dance to tonight."

"So do I," the Viscount said. "Of course there are many places in which we could dance, but I feel that they would expect me to talk very seriously about the Russian situation."

The Princess gave a cry.

"Oh, not again! We have had it over and over, day after day, and surely you do not have to repeat all you have heard from the Hungarians. It will be too boring!"

"That is my job," the Viscount said.

She put out her hand to hold on to him.

"Are you telling me that when they send you abroad again, I will not be able to go with you?"

He knew by the way she spoke how much the idea upset her.

"That is something I have no intention of doing in the future," he said. "I am sure I can find plenty to do at home."

He was, however, not quite certain if this was possible.

He had always been busy with his work as a Diplomat.

He could not imagine having nothing to do except attending Social functions, which he invariably found boring.

The house in London where he lived belonged to his Father.

But, as the Earl seldom left the country, he had begun to think of it entirely as his own.

He had his horses in training at Newmarket.

Yet, when he visited them, he either stayed with a friend or in a Hotel and had no country-house of his own.

He could see this was a new problem he had not faced before.

As a married man who wanted to be with his wife, it would be difficult to be at the "beck and call" of Lord Granville as he had been in the past.

It had been so easy then to move to some obscure part of the world at only a few hours' notice.

He could slip over to Paris to have a word with the Ambassador without being sure what day he would return.

Yet if he had to give that up, he knew he would have no regrets.

Yentha would fill his life so that he would not miss the excitement and what he had been doing these past years.

He supposed that inevitably there would be something to take its place.

The difficulty was that at the moment he was not sure what it was.

They arrived at the British Embassy.

As the Viscount had stayed there so often, the Servants greeted him respectfully as an old friend.

An Aide-de-Camp came hurrying to tell the Viscount that the Ambassador was eager to see him immediately.

The young man looked with surprise at Yentha, and the Viscount said:

"Let me introduce you to my wife. I know His Excellency is not aware of my marriage. Perhaps you will be kind enough to arrange our accommodation which I know will be different to what I would have as a bachelor."

"Yes, of course! Of course, My Lord," the ADC said in rather a flutter. "I will see to it at once."

He hurried away.

The Viscount walked towards a Sitting-Room.

He knew where he would be expected to wait until he was ushered into the presence of the Ambassador.

He was, however, concerned with quite another matter which he had not mentioned to Yentha.

It was, he knew, important from Lord Granville's point of view.

Yet he was aware that he should speak to the Ambassador first.

At last, after what seemed a quite unnecessary delay, the ADC appeared.

"His Excellency is ready to see you, My Lord," he said.

The Viscount replied:

"As I have business to discuss with His Excellency, I think my wife should go upstairs to rest. I will, of course, join her as soon as possible."

The last words were really directed towards Yentha.

She smiled at him to show she understood what he was trying to do.

"I will be as quick as I can," he said in a low voice.

As he took her hand, he felt her fingers squeeze his.

He then walked towards the Ambassador's room, and without waiting to be announced, walked in.

The Ambassador was an elderly man.

He rose from his desk.

"It is nice to see you, Bredon!" he said. "I have news for you which has been awaiting your arrival."

"Before we do anything private," the Viscount said, "I think you will understand that I felt I should send a code to London with regard to Pandjeh."

The Ambassador stiffened.

"You know about Pandjeh?"

"I have information which should be conveyed immediately to Lord Granville," the Viscount said. "But I would like to hear first exactly what you know here."

"What we have been told," the Ambassador said, sitting down, "is that the Russians have reached Pandjeh and there is a vague and unconfirmed story, despite the Tsar's promises that they will not attack the Fort, that they have taken it."

"That is correct," the Viscount said.

"I cannot believe it!" the Ambassador exclaimed. "How is it possible after the Tsar's promise that they would not fight the Afghans, although they have been gradually closing in on Pandjeh!"

"I can give you the whole story," the Viscount replied. "It was a trick, which is exactly what might be expected of the Russians. But I think first it should be sent to London."

"Yes, of course! Of course!" the Ambassador agreed.

He was obviously shaken by what the Viscount had said to him.

He told the ADC to take him immediately to the Cable Office.

The British had instituted in 1870 a cable system which more or less covered the world.

It was of vital importance for India, as it went through Bombay.

Actually, most of the cable traffic went by land to Marseilles, picking up a big cable line in Malta.

They were used in cities and through the British Embassy only when it was a question of emergency.

The Viscount was shown into a small room where he was given a Code Book.

It was kept secret from everyone who was not in a very high position.

He sent a cable through to Lord Granville. He said he had information that was correct and above suspicion that Pandjeh had been seized and the Garrison butchered by the Russians.

When he had sent it, he knew that the situation would now be of the utmost gravity.

There would be no doubt that most people, including the Foreign Diplomats in London, would now assume that War between the two Great Powers was inevitable.

He could imagine the fury of Mr. Gladstone, the Prime Minister, he who had been made a fool of not only by the Russian Generals but by the Tsar himself.

The only hope might lie with the Afghans.

But one could not be completely sure which way they would jump.

Thinking deeply, the Viscount went back to the Ambassador's room.

"I can hardly believe that this is really true," he said as the Viscount entered. "Are you quite sure you can trust your information?"

"I can do that," the Viscount said. "We can only hope and pray that in some way War can be prevented."

"Unfortunately, we have a long list," the Ambassador said, "of St. Petersburg's record of broken pledges. It is impossible to trust the Russians."

"I know that only too well," the Viscount replied.

There was silence for a moment.

Then the Ambassador said:

"Now we must get down to your news. I am afraid you may be upset by what I have to impart to you."

The Viscount wondered what it could be, and the Ambassador said:

"I was told a few days ago, when actually you were

137

moving out of St. Petersburg, that your Father, the Earl, had died."

"He died?" the Viscount exclaimed.

It was not actually a surprise, because his Father had been in very poor health for a long time.

But he had somehow not expected his death to come so quickly.

"I understand," the Ambassador went on, "that Lord Granville thought it a mistake to inform you of your bereavement while you were still on a very important mission."

He paused before he added:

"I can only express my sympathy and tell you how sorry I am that you should receive this news immediately on your return."

As the Viscount did not speak, he continued:

"I think I am right in saying that as you could not be reached, your Father was to be buried yesterday."

"It has certainly been a shock," the Viscount said. "Even though we have all been expecting it for some time. He disliked being an invalid and would, I think, have been glad to be rid of this world."

"You are being very brave about it," the Ambassador said. "I also understand from what my *Aide-de-Camp* has told me that you arrived with your wife."

The Viscount nodded.

"I was married while I was away, and though it might have annoyed my Father, the ceremony took place in a foreign country without his knowledge."

He made a gesture with his hand and went on:

"There is no need now for me to make explanations, but it is essential for the moment that no-one except yourself need be aware of my marriage until I am back in England and can announce it in the proper manner."

"I understand," the Ambassador said, "and of course I am very pleased to be able to entertain your wife while you are here, but I imagine you will leave tomorrow, so that you can cope with the things that are waiting for you when you get home."

"Of course, and thank you for your help," the Viscount said.

He left the Ambassador's room.

He was thinking that everything seemed to happen to him in the most unexpected and unusual manner.

He walked slowly up the stairs to where he was told that Yentha would be waiting for him.

He thought that now his Father was dead, everything was changed.

As the Earl of Bredonhurst, his position would be very different from that of a young Diplomat who was interested in his work.

His Father's Estate was enormous and inevitably required a great deal of attention.

He would also, as the Earl of Bredonhurst, be a Member of the House of Lords.

He had not expected to be a senior Statesman there until he was much older.

Yet it would be another way of helping Lord Granville with the very difficult problems that were happening in the world outside.

"At least my voice will be heard," Lyle told himself with a feeling of satisfaction.

The Servant who led him upstairs stopped at a door on the first floor and knocked.

Lyle heard his wife's voice and went in.

Yentha was undressed.

She was standing near the window, wearing only a diaphanous nightgown in which she had intended to rest.

As Lyle entered, she turned round.

When she saw who it was, she gave a cry of joy and ran across the room to fling herself into his arms.

There was a great deal he wanted to tell her.

Instead, he found himself kissing her wildly.

As she returned his kisses, with her arms around his neck, it was impossible to speak.

He knew only that for the moment the Russians,

the fate of Pandjeh, and the question of War were not important.

Nor did he remember he was no longer a Viscount but an Earl.

All that mattered was Yentha!

Yentha and their love.

chapter seven

WHEN he could think a little more clearly, Lyle said:

"I have something to tell you, Darling."

The way he spoke made Yentha stiffen for a moment and look at him apprehensively.

"What is it?" she asked.

"The Ambassador has just told me," he replied, "that my Father died when I was in St. Petersburg."

"He . . . he . . . is . . . dead!" she said almost beneath her breath. "Does that mean . . . that you do . . . not want . . . me anymore?"

Her husband stared at her.

"How could you think such a thing?" he asked. "I want you anyway, but particularly now that I have more responsibility."

He felt her relax.

She gave a sigh of relief, and he said:

"I love you! How could you imagine for a moment that I could manage my life without you?"

"Do you . . . really mean . . . that?" she asked. "I am sorry . . . very sorry . . . about your Father."

"I think in a way he would be glad to go," Lyle said. "He had been ill for a long time, and he hated thinking he could not do the things he used to do, like shooting and fishing."

"But it is always sad when we lose someone we

love and who is part of us," Yentha said softly.

"I knew you would understand," Lyle replied.

There was a little silence, then Yentha said:

"You know, Darling, you promised that I could pray at the Stephanskirche. I think now we ought to pray for ... your Father and ... also to ... thank God for ... us."

"We will do that," Lyle agreed.

He thought for a moment and then went on:

"We do not wish to make conversation with strangers who will undoubtedly be dining here tonight. I will tell the Ambassador that I am taking you out to Dinner."

"We ... can be ... alone?" Yentha asked.

"Yes, alone!" Lyle said. "And it will be in a Restaurant."

"I have never dined alone with a man," Yentha replied, "and of course not in a Restaurant."

"Then it will be a new experience," Lyle answered. "First we will go to the Madeleine and say a prayer, as you wish to do."

He kissed her gently.

Then he went to find the Ambassador's Secretary to tell him what his plans were.

"I am very sorry, My Lord, to hear the bad news of your Father," the Secretary said.

"It is something I did not expect," Lyle replied.

"Is there anything I can do for you?" the Secretary asked. "Perhaps Her Ladyship wants something black to wear?"

Lyle stared at him.

It never occurred to him that Yentha should be in mourning.

Then he thought it very unlikely, in the small amount of clothes she had brought with her when she was running away from the Tsar, there would be anything black.

"I am glad you mentioned this," he said to the Secretary. "As I shall have to buy my wife a black gown, we had better catch the later train to Calais instead of the earlier one."

"I will arrange it, My Lord," the Secretary answered.

Lyle went upstairs again.

"I have just spoken to His Excellency's Secretary," he said to Yentha, "and he suggested, with what I thought was unexpected common-sense, that you will require some black clothes."

"I never thought of it!" Yentha exclaimed. "And as you might imagine, I very seldom wear black."

"Then we will go to buy your trousseau," Lyle said as he smiled. "But it will not be in the colours that I have always thought of you as wearing."

"It will be very exciting to have some dresses from Paris," Yentha said. "But are you sure that you can afford it?"

Lyle smiled to himself.

He realised that now his Father was dead, he was a very rich man.

He had always been afraid that if he was not careful he would be married for his money if not for his title.

He thought, with her unusual beauty, it would be a joy in the future to dress Yentha in the most attractive clothes it was possible to find.

"I was just thinking," she said, "that I do not possess a black gown to wear tonight."

"We shall see no-one who will know us," Lyle replied. "We will start mourning tomorrow, when I have bought you a gown in the Rue de la Paix."

He went to his own room to bathe and change.

He told Bates about his Father.

"Well, that means things'll be a bit different fer yer, M'Lord, in the future," Bates said, "an' I suppose we'll be going to yer country-house as soon as us gets home?"

"Yes, of course," Lyle replied. "But I am very anxious, Bates, that no-one there should know that my wife has Russian blood in her. I trust you, to say nothing about how she came into my life and that the

Third Section has been following her."

"Yer can trust me, M'Lord," Bates said. "Mum is me second name and yer knows I never talks."

"Yes, I know that, Bates. But people will be naturally curious and they will ask you a lot of questions."

"An' them that asks no questions gets no lies!"

It was a typical Bates remark, and Lyle smiled.

Then, when he lay in his bath, he was thinking that once again he had to be clever where Yentha was concerned.

It would be a great mistake at this moment, when England and Russia were at "daggers drawn," for anyone to have the slightest idea she was Russian.

When he went to Yentha's room, he was still thinking how cleverly he could arrange things.

She was dressed. He appreciated that although her gown was not black, it was not a very bright colour.

The silk cape she wore round her shoulders was a deep blue.

"Do I look all right?" she asked.

He saw that she had remembered, though he had not told her, that women in Paris who dined out wore hats.

What she had done, obviously not having one that was suitable, was to tie a blue ribbon round her hair which matched her cape.

She had pinned on it the feathers of a Bird of Paradise.

The result was very attractive.

She had actually pushed the feathers into her trunk at the last moment, before she had left St. Petersburg.

Because they were so pretty, she thought it was a mistake to leave them behind.

Now they were exactly what she wanted for the evening to cover her dark hair.

She knew, from the expression in her husband's eyes, that he thought it became her.

"Now," he said, "we start our evening together. I hope, my Darling, you will enjoy it."

"I cannot imagine anything more exciting than to be in Paris and with you," she said. "I am only afraid that you will miss the wild gaieties which I am sure you enjoyed when you were here as a bachelor."

Lyle thought some of them had, in fact, been very wild.

But he knew that at the moment there was nothing he wanted more than to be alone with Yentha.

To feel her love vibrating from her which seemed to get stronger every moment they were together was wonderful.

They went down the Embassy stairs hand in hand.

The carriage which had been ordered by the Secretary was waiting for them.

Lyle told the *Major Domo* who assisted them into it that they were to go first to the Madelcine.

He thought the man looked at him in surprise.

The Madeleine was only a very short distance away.

He could have gone to the British Embassy Church, which was nearer.

But he thought Yentha would appreciate the beauty and sanctity of the Madeleine.

As they climbed up the long steps which led into it, they could hear the organ playing very softly.

Then there was the scent of incense and an atmosphere of sanctity which seemed to envelop them.

Lyle remembered discussing the Madeleine with a friend when he was last in Paris.

He had been told it was the only Church in Paris that had a Chapel dedicated to St. Joseph, who was the Patron Saint of marriages.

His friend had actually said where it was placed, on the right-hand side as one entered, by the West Door.

Lyle drew Yentha towards it.

"This is where we pray, my Darling," he said, "that our marriage will be happy and last forever."

He saw the light in her eyes.

When she knelt down in front of the altar, he joined her.

He prayed as he had not prayed since he was a small boy.

He thought, as he did so, that it was something he had never expected to do in Paris, of all places.

Yet he knew that this was the first step in the new life that lay ahead of him.

He had never thought of it before.

But now he knew that in his heart he had always wanted his wife to be religious.

She should worship God and teach his children, when he had them, to pray as his Mother had taught him.

He could not imagine any other woman who had been of importance in his life wishing on her first night in Paris to visit the Madeleine.

She would have rather been at some exciting party, at which she could obtain a great number of fulsome compliments.

He glanced at Yentha kneeling beside him.

He thought nothing could be more beautiful than her face raised towards the altar with her eyes shut.

Her fingers were touching each other in the age-old attitude of prayer.

'This,' he thought, 'is exactly how my wife and the future Mother of my children should look.'

He had never realised it until that moment.

When they rose and walked back to the West Door, he thought there was an expression on Yentha's face as if she had been spiritually uplifted and felt she was very near to God.

As they got into the carriage again, she did not speak, but slipped her hand into her husband's.

He had told the Footman on the box to take them to a very quiet Restaurant where he knew the food was exceptionally good.

It was therefore patronised by gourmets and conoisseurs of wine.

It was, in fact, too expensive and too exclusive for those who merely wanted to enjoy the *joie de vivre* of Paris.

The best sofa-table had been engaged for them.

When they sat down, Lyle realised there were only a dozen other people in the Restaurant.

They were all more or less middle-aged.

Nevertheless, the women were very smartly dressed and Yentha was glad that Lyle would not be ashamed of her appearance.

Because it was expected of him, he took a long time choosing a delicious Dinner and the wines which were suitable to each course.

Then, when the *Mâitre d'Hôtel* had moved away, he said to Yentha:

"Here is some of the best food in Paris, and, I hope, my Darling, you will appreciate it."

"I should be very shocked at myself if I did not," Yentha replied. "Though I doubt if, because you are so grand, I shall ever be allowed to cook for you. I can, however, do a number of very special dishes which were Papa's favourites."

Lyle smiled.

"I am always thinking that you have new talents," he said, "and that in itself is something to look forward to."

He paused and then went on:

"Of course you shall cook for me, and perhaps we can have a second Honeymoon just by ourselves in some part of the country where no-one will disturb us."

Yentha clasped her hands together.

"You know I would love that more than anything else! I wish we could do it now."

"So do I," Lyle said. "But we have to go home first because, as you will understand, someone has to give orders now that my Father is dead, and that must be me."

"You will . . . let . . . me help . . . you?" Yentha asked.

"You will have to," he answered. "I cannot do

everything myself, and when you see Bredon Hall you will understand why there is so much to do."

He did not, however, want to make her apprehensive of what lay ahead.

He therefore talked of other things.

But inevitably, because they were together and so very much in love, every subject seemed eventually to get back to themselves.

Then, as they looked into each other's eyes, it was impossible to remember what they had been saying.

Their thoughts said what was in their hearts.

When Dinner was finished, and it was a very delicious one, the carriage was waiting.

Yentha thought that they would go back to the Embassy.

Instead, on Lyle's instructions they drove along the banks of the Seine.

They saw the lights on the great river and the barges going up and down.

The stars overhead were making everything enchanting.

"It is so lovely," Yentha said.

Lyle had had the hood of the carriage taken down so that they could see better.

At one place they stopped and went down the steps which led to the water's edge.

"This is Paris," he said. "I want you to enjoy it as much as I do, so that we come here again when we want to escape the responsibility of all the things we have to do in England."

He was thinking as he spoke that Paris had always seemed to him not only a place of gaiety, but love.

Now the love he had sensed on the very air itself seemed to him to be part of their happiness.

He knew Yentha felt the same.

He kissed her in the shadows of a bridge.

Then they climbed up the steps again and got back into the carriage.

As they returned to the Embassy, Lyle was aware

that Yentha's heart was beating.

She wanted him as much as he wanted her.

The next morning, without having to see the Ambassador, they managed to get away quickly after breakfast.

Lyle gave the Coachman an address in the *Rue de la Paix*.

He knew that the shop to which he was taking Yentha was kept by one of the most distinguished dress Designers.

He had followed the example set by Frederick Worth, an Englishman who had made the women of Paris the smartest in the whole of Europe.

Lyle had actually visited the shop with a very lovely lady.

She had asked him to give her a gown as a present.

The Frenchmen always enjoyed choosing a woman's dress, and making sure it really became her.

Lyle, however, had never actually visited a dressmaker in any city before.

He had, however, found it quite amusing.

It was surprising the trouble the Designer took not just selling a gown but in making certain it was a perfect frame for the woman who was wearing it.

A little bit was added here, and a little more taken off there!

The Designer seemed to give not only his mind but his heart to what he was creating.

When the shop heard that Yentha would require only some black gowns they did not commiserate with her, nor did they think it was wrong for her to wear black when her hair was dark.

Instead, they produced the most exquisite gowns that only the French could have created.

There was something so *chic* about each one that the onlooker forgot the colour.

Lyle was aware that it displayed the beauty of Yentha's soft curves and the elegance of her very small waist.

Some of the gowns had a touch of white, which relieved the black and made it seem more of a provocation than a penalty.

Then, thinking that there would be no need for Yentha to be in mourning for too long, Lyle ordered some gowns that were half-mourning:

A soft mauve which made her look exquisitely beautiful.

A grey that was almost silver that shimmered when she moved.

A white dress embroidered all over with *diamanté* was for her to wear at a Ball.

Yentha was entranced with each one.

If Lyle had wished to be thanked, he knew that the excitement in her eyes and the little exclamations that came from her lips were what he wanted to hear.

They took the gowns which were ready with them.

They arranged for the rest to be sent to England as soon as possible.

There were several hats which went with the gowns.

Those were placed in a hat-box to travel with them.

As they went back to the Embassy, Lyle was aware that time was passing.

They would soon have to leave for the *Gare du Nord*.

As soon as they entered the British Embassy the Ambassador's Secretary came hurrying towards them.

"There are two men to see you, My Lord," he said. "I think they are Russians, but they would not give their names. They insist that their business with you is important."

As he spoke, Lyle felt Yentha clutch his arm.

He put his hand over hers and said:

"Leave this to me, my Darling! Go upstairs and get ready to leave for the Station."

"You will . . . be . . . careful," she whispered.

"Of course," he answered. "Do not worry!"

He saw the fear in her eyes as she turned away.

When she was out of earshot, he said to the Secretary:

"I want a revolver. There is one in my bedroom, but it will save time if you have one handy."

"Yes, we have one," the Secretary said. "I hope there is not going to be any trouble."

"I hope not, too," Lyle replied.

The Secretary hurried and came back a few minutes later with a revolver.

Lyle looked to see if it was loaded, then put it in his pocket.

As he knew in which room the Russians would be waiting, he walked into it without being announced.

One glance at the two men waiting for him told him that he had never seen them before.

He imagined that they had been instructed to keep watch in Paris for Yentha.

They might or might not know the other Russians had disappeared in Vienna.

He was only guessing.

At the same time, he remembered how often he had heard that the Third Section never gave up.

They always find their man in the end!

The words seemed to be drumming in his ears.

As he entered the room slowly, without haste, he carried himself with a dignity that was very impressive.

It made him, in fact, seem older than he was.

The Russians, who had been sitting down, rose and bowed to him.

Lyle just stood looking at them in a somewhat intimidating manner, until one of them said:

"You the Viscount Bredon?"

He mispronounced the name, and it was obvious that his English was not very good.

Slowly, so that both men could understand, Lyle replied:

"No! I am the Earl of Bredonhurst!"

There was a silence, then the same man who had spoken before said:

"It is Viscount we come to see!"

It was then almost as if he had been helped by a Power outside himself that Lyle knew what the answer should be.

Still speaking very slowly and impressively, he said:

"The Viscount Bredon no longer exists!"

Both men listening stared at him in astonishment.

Then they spoke to each other quickly and *sotto voce* so that Lyle could not follow what they said.

Then one of them said the Russian word for "dead," and he knew what they were thinking.

The first man who had spoken turned again to face him.

"Can you tell, *Monsieur*," he said, "where we find the Princess Yentha Kerenska?"

"The Princess also no longer exists!" Lyle replied.

The two Russians looked at each other and were obviously pleased by the news.

Then the spokesman said:

"We very grateful, *Monsieur*, now we know what happened we ask no more!"

Almost as if he were being prompted, Lyle enquired:

"Will you be returning to St. Petersburg?"

"Yes! Yes, *Monsieur*," the Russian replied eagerly. "We go now! Business in Paris finish!"

"Then I can only wish you," Lyle said, "*bon voyage!*"

He turned as he spoke and went from the room.

As he walked across the hall, he knew at last the fear and terror Yentha had felt since she left St. Petersburg was over.

Unless anything went really wrong—and there was no reason why it should—the Russians who had been instructed to wait for them in Paris believed her to be dead.

They would now return to tell the Tsar their search had ended.

There was no reason why he should question it, especially at this moment, when he was so involved with the distinct possibility of War with Great Britain.

Lyle was certain he would accept what he heard as quite unimportant.

He would then forget the very existence of the young girl who had disobeyed his orders.

Lyle thought that once again God had helped them.

He knew that was what Yentha would think.

When he entered the bedroom she was waiting for him.

He saw by the expression in her eyes how frightened she was.

When he shut the door behind him, she asked in a voice he could hardly hear:

"What . . . has . . . happened?"

He threw open his arms.

"It is all over, my Darling. We have won completely and absolutely. It is something you need never think of again."

She went towards him, and he held her close against him.

"I . . . cannot . . . understand," she murmured.

"I will tell you exactly what happened," he said. "But first of all tell me you love me and promise you will stop being frightened because in the new life you and I are going to spend together there will be no fear!"

"H-how . . . is that . . . possible? What did . . . the Russians want? H-how . . . could they . . . have found us . . . here?"

Very gently, holding her close to him, Lyle explained what had occurred.

He told her how he was convinced that the Russians believed that she was dead.

It was then she cried.

Tears of happiness ran down her cheeks and Lyle kissed them away.

"It cannot be true!" she sobbed. "I have been frightened for . . . so long. Now you really . . . think the Tsar will . . . forget about . . . me?"

"I think, my Darling," Lyle said, "he has far more important things to think about. As far as I am concerned, I can think only of you!"

"We are . . . free! We are . . . free!" the Princess cried.

She put her arms around his neck and kissed him, and he kissed her.

Then abruptly he remembered that time was passing and they had to get to England.

Yentha washed away the tears and put on one of her pretty new hats. Lyle hurried the Servants to take the luggage downstairs.

They said a hasty "good-bye" to the Ambassador and set off for the Station.

Fortunately, the Embassy had already arranged for their accommodation.

Naturally, it was the best available on the train.

They were locked in their compartment so that no-one could join them.

A large hamper of food was provided from the Embassy kitchens, and there was also a bouquet of flowers for Yentha.

"They have done their best," Lyle said as the train moved out of the *Gare du Nord*.

"I enjoyed my first visit to Paris," Yentha said. "Please, Darling Lyle, can we go another time, and enjoy it even more?"

"We will go this time next year, if not before," Lyle promised.

Then he said:

"Now we are starting a new chapter in a new book and in a new life. We have to remember that not only as far as the Russians are concerned, but also the English, we are two different people."

Yentha looked at him a little worriedly.

"How . . . different?" she enquired.

"You are now the Countess of Bredonhurst," her

husband replied, "and as I am the Earl, we have to forget that the two people who have been sought by the Third Section ever existed."

"Is that really possible?" Yentha enquired.

"I think it is," Lyle replied. "First of all, I have decided we will go straight to Bredonhurst Hall and see what we have to do there. As we are in mourning, we need not see our neighbours and as little as possible of my family."

He could tell by the puzzled expression on her face that Yentha was listening.

"Because we are in deep mourning," he went on, "we will explain it is a mistake to announce our wedding publicly for perhaps two months. By then we shall have been in touch with your Grandfather, and I am quite certain you will find he will welcome the Countess of Bredonhurst into the family."

"He was very . . . angry with . . . Mama," Yentha murmured.

"That is as may be!" Lyle replied. "But he is well aware that we are, in fact, an older and more important family than his."

"But he is a Duke!" Yentha exclaimed.

"Only the fourth Duke of Wilthorp," was the reply, "and I am the twelfth Earl of Bredonhurst."

Yentha laughed.

"Then you are certainly very important, Darling, and I will be very, very respectful to you."

"What matters," Lyle said, "is that they should consider you important, as I am quite certain they will. There is no need for anyone to talk about your Father. Your Mother was the daughter of the Duke, and because she lived abroad for nearly twenty years, there will be very few people left to remember her. Those who do, knowing your Grandfather's feelings, will be careful not to mention it."

Yentha clapped her hands.

"You have thought it all out. I think it is very clever. Yet all that really matters to me is that you love me and that you are . . . not ashamed . . . of me."

"How could I be?" Lyle asked.

He reached out to pull her into his arms.

Then their hearts seemed to race like the turning wheels of the train beneath them.

It was two days later that the Earl and Countess of Bredonhurst arrived at their ancestral home in Huntingdonshire.

Her first glance at the house as they drove up the long drive made Yentha think it seemed enormous.

It was almost too big for only two people.

Yet, as Lyle was aware, she was used to Palaces and she was therefore not over-awed as so many people were by Bredonhurst Hall.

She was intrigued, as he thought she would be, only by the display of magnificent pictures.

They had been collected down the centuries.

There were treasures to be found in every room which had been added to by every generation.

A large number of Servants was waiting in the Hall when the Earl and Countess arrived.

The Viscount liked the way Yentha shook hands with everybody and managed to have something different to say to each one.

He knew, in fact, that at first sight she had conquered those who had served his family for years.

He was certain it was something she would continue to do to anyone who came to the house.

There was so much to see and so much to talk about.

They seemed to become almost breathless when they dined in the smaller Dining-Room which was more intimate than the huge Banqueting Hall.

"Tomorrow," Lyle said, "we will do a tour of the house. You must see the kitchens where this very delicious food has come from."

"I was just thinking how good it was," Yentha said.

"The Cook," Lyle answered, "has been here ever since I was a small boy. She has given me all the dishes I used to ask for in the holidays, and she has not forgotten one."

"I am glad you told me," Yentha said. "I will remember tomorrow to congratulate her on them."

"I thought you would," he replied, "and we have also to make a tour of the Estate. It is something we cannot do in one day, but will take us the best part of a week."

He smiled at the surprise on her face and went on:

"Every Farmer will want to see me, and every Farmer's wife will admire you."

"I can see there is a great deal to do," Yentha replied. "But if we do it together it will be very exciting and exactly what I . . . wanted for . . . you."

"For me?" he enquired.

"Do you not understand," Yentha said, "how wonderful it is that you have not got to go back on those frightening Diplomatic Missions or alternatively be bored in a London house because you would not have enough to do."

Lyle knew this was true, and it was what he thought himself.

He had to admit that Fate had been very kind.

He had been given a great many new things to occupy his mind even before he made his entry into the House of Lords.

He had also not told Yentha yet, but he had a traditional place at Court.

Yentha was now a traditional Lady-of-the-Bedchamber to the Queen.

He did not want to frighten her.

Yet he was well aware that the duties they would have to perform for their County were inclined to be overwhelming.

His Father had been the Lord Lieutenant of Huntingdonshire, a position which would now be waiting for him.

He would also be expected to be the Patron of innumerable Charities, Schools, and Universities.

There was a whole list waiting for him on his desk.

"Before we do anything else," he said when the Servants had left the room, "we have to be married."

Yentha laughed.

"That sounds as if we were not married already. That would definitely shock everybody."

"I have already told my Secretary I wished to see the Vicar, who is also my Private Chaplain," Lyle said, "and tomorrow evening, when we will be alone, and there is no chance of being disturbed by someone dropping in, we will be married in the Chapel."

His voice was serious as he added:

"It is something we can remember for the rest of our lives."

Yentha made a little sound of delight.

"That is what I wanted," she said. "You can be quite sure, Darling, that I shall always remember it."

She put her hand over his as she continued:

"I know that it was our prayers that brought us here so safely, and those very special ones we made in the Madeleine, after the last of the Russians who were . . . following us went . . . back to . . . St. Petersburg."

"That is exactly what I have been thinking," Lyle said, "and of course the end of the story will be that we lived happily ever afterwards."

Yentha smiled at him in a way which made him think she was even more beautiful than she had been a moment before.

The following morning they were beset by people on the Estate wishing to talk, complain, beg, and, of course, congratulate them.

They were both thinking what the night would bring.

"Only Lyle," Yentha told herself later, "could have thought of making me happy in such a unique manner."

At the same time, he was making sure it was

something she would always remember.

They had a very early Dinner.

When it was finished, Lyle said:

"The Parson will be arriving shortly, so go upstairs and you will find something special is waiting for you."

Curious, but asking no questions because she felt that he did not want her to, Yentha ran up to her bedroom.

The old Housekeeper who had been at the Hall for over forty years, was waiting there.

"His Lordship told me, My Lady," she said, "you're to have a Service of Blessing in the Chapel tonight. That's something that's pleased us all."

Yentha smiled, and the Housekeeper went on:

"His Lordship's asked me to find a very special gown for you, and I have several from which you are to choose."

She pointed towards the bed.

"I thinks," she went on, "the prettiest is the one from the reign of Queen Anne. But there's one that is a little earlier and another that's later."

Yentha had thought she would have to be married in the black evening gown she had bought in Paris.

She put on the while lace gown with delight.

She found that it wanted little alteration to fit her.

Then the Housekeeper brought to her a magnificent lace veil which had been used by the Brides of Bredonhurst for four hundred years.

To go over it, and this Yentha thought was particularly clever of Lyle, was a special tiara.

It was made of stars.

It was not so large and impressive as the one she had worn of her Mother's.

Nor was it, she learnt later, as grand as the traditional tiara the Countesses of Bredonhurst wore at the Opening of Parliament.

But stars meant something very special to her and Lyle.

As she put the tiara on her head, the stars were coming out in the sky.

She was sure that she could feel them moving in her breast.

The bouquet that was waiting for her was of Madonna Lilies.

When she went down the stairs, Lyle was waiting for her in the Hall.

He was wearing more decorations than Yentha was expecting him to have.

He looked so handsome that she could hardly believe he was real.

Without speaking, he gave her his arm.

They moved slowly down the long passage which led to the Chapel.

It had been built when the house was originally started in the reign of Mary Tudor.

As they drew near, Yentha could hear an organ was playing.

When she entered, she saw the Chapel for the first time.

She had known, when Lyle had taken her round the house, that he had deliberately abstained from taking her to the Chapel.

It was massed with flowers, but not so many as to hide the beauty of the carvings, the exquisitely painted ceiling, and the stained-glass windows.

There were monuments to the past Earls and Countesses.

Yentha thought that one day there would be one for her, and for the man who had given her such unbelievable happiness.

She knew that the Chapel would always mean something very special to her, not only because she had been married in it, but it was here she could pray for their love.

She could also pray for a solution to any of the problems which were bound to arise in their lives sooner or later.

The Parson was waiting for them.

When they reached him, he started, as Yentha hoped he would, the Marriage Service.

He spoke very simply and movingly.

She felt they were not alone in the Chapel. Her Father and Mother were there.

She was sure it was they who had brought her through every danger to a haven of peace.

Then, when she and Lyle knelt for the Blessing, Yentha felt as if the Light of God encircled them.

It was a sign that He would protect them, not only now but all through their lives.

It was all very moving.

When finally they went upstairs, as Lyle shut the door behind him Yentha said:

"Thank you! Thank you, Darling! It is something I shall always remember. It was for me a perfect wedding."

"For me, too," Lyle answered in a deep voice. "Now we are really married, it will be impossible for you to escape from me."

"Do you think I want to?" Yentha asked. "I thought, when we were being Blessed, that no-one could be as lucky as you and I."

"I thought the same," he said.

He walked across the room and pulled back the curtains.

Outside, the sky was brilliant with stars.

The moon which had protected them in Vienna threw a silver light into the bedroom.

Lyle pulled off his tight-fitting coat and threw it on a chair.

Then, very gently, he removed the star tiara from his wife's head.

"It is so lovely," she said. "How could you have anything so perfect which meant so much to us both?"

"It has been in my family for years," Lyle said. "I intend to buy you a ring to go with it, which, of course, will be in the shape of a star.''

''What I really want are your kisses,'' Yentha said.

''And they are yours, now and forever,'' Lyle replied.

As she moved into his arms, she felt him undoing the buttons at the back of her wedding gown.

It fell to the ground with a little shimmer.

He lifted her up in his arms.

''When you carry me,'' she whispered, ''I think of how you lifted me so quickly into the luggage rack to hide from the Russians.''

''Forget them! And everything about them!'' Lyle ordered. ''That is all in the past, and now tomorrow lies ahead of us, filled with excitement!''

He kissed her hair before he said:

''There is a great deal to do, and perhaps some problems. But we will solve them as we solved those in the past, not only with our brains, but, as you believe, my Darling, with the help of God.''

''He has helped us,'' Yentha whispered.

Lyle had put her down on the bed.

Then, as she looked at him, the moonlight seemed to make a special halo around him.

It was as if once again he was being Blessed and protected by Heaven itself.

Then, as he joined her, she knew that this was true.

They had passed through deep waters and they had survived.

Only God could have brought them together and joined them so completely, so that they were no longer two people but one.

As Lyle kissed her, Yentha prayed that she might have many children who would carry on the work he had done for England.

Lyle was touching her and she felt herself quiver.

Then the stars glittered in her heart and turned into flames of fire.

As they reached towards the peaks of ecstasy, they knew their love would sustain and protect them, not only for this life but for many lives to come.

ABOUT THE AUTHOR

Barbara Cartland, the world's most famous romantic novelist, who is also an historian, playwright, lecturer, political speaker and television personality, has now written 617 books and sold over six hundred and twenty million copies all over the world.

She has also had many historical works published and has written four autobiographies as well as the biographies of her mother and that of her brother, Ronald Cartland, who was the first Member of Parliament to be killed in the last war. This book has a preface by Sir Winston Churchill and has been republished with an introduction by Sir Arthur Bryant.

Love at the Helm, a novel written with the help and inspiration of the late Earl Mountbatten of Burma, Great Uncle of His Royal Highness, The Prince of Wales, is being sold for the Mountbatten Memorial Trust.

She has broken the world record for the last twenty-one years by writing an average of twenty-three books a year. In the *Guinness Book of World Records* she is listed as the world's top-selling author.

Miss Cartland in 1987 sang an Album of Love Songs with the Royal Philharmonic Orchestra.

In private life Barbara Cartland, who is a Dame of the Order of St. John of Jerusalem and Chairman of the St. John Council in Hertfordshire, has fought for better conditions and salaries for Midwives and Nurses.

She championed the cause for the Elderly in 1956, invoking a Government Enquiry into the "Housing Condition of Old People."

In 1962 she had the Law of England changed so that Local Authorities had to provide camps for their own Gypsies. This has meant that since then thousands and thousands of Gypsy children have been able to go to School, which they had never been able to do in the past, as their caravans were moved every twenty-four hours by the Police.

There are now fifteen camps in Hertfordshire and Barbara Cartland has her own Romany Gypsy Camp called "Barbaraville" by the Gypsies.

Her designs "Decorating with Love" are being sold all over the U.S.A. and the National Home Fashions League made her, in 1981, "Woman of Achievement."

She is unique in that she was one and two in the Dalton list of Best Sellers, and one week had four books in the top twenty.

Barbara Cartland's book *Getting Older, Growing Younger* has been published in Great Britain and the U.S.A. and her fifth cookery book, *The Romance of Food*, is now being used by the House of Commons.

In 1984 she received at Kennedy Airport

America's Bishop Wright Air Industry Award for her contribution to the development of aviation. In 1931 she and two R.A.F. Officers thought of, and carried, the first aeroplane-towed glider airmail.

During the War she was Chief Lady Welfare Officer in Bedfordshire, looking after 20,000 Servicemen and -women. She thought of having a pool of Wedding Dresses at the War Office so a Service Bride could hire a gown for the day.

She bought 1,000 gowns without coupons for the A.T.S., the W.A.A.F.s and the W.R.E.N.S. In 1945 Barbara Cartland received the Certificate of Merit from Eastern Command.

In 1964 Barbara Cartland founded the National Association for Health of which she is the President, as a front for all the Health Stores and for any product made as alternative medicine.

This is now a £65 million turnover a year, with one-third going in export.

In January 1968 she received *La Médeille de Vermeil de la Ville de Paris*. This is the highest award to be given in France by the City of Paris. She has sold 30 million books in France.

In March 1988 Barbara Cartland was asked by the Indian Government to open their Health Resort outside Delhi. This is almost the largest Health Resort in the world.

Barbara Cartland was received with great enthusiasm by her fans, who feted her at a reception in the City, and she received the gift of an embossed plate from the Government.

Barbara Cartland was made a Dame of the Order of the British Empire in the 1991 New

Year's Honours List by Her Majesty, The Queen, for her contribution to Literature and also for her years of work for the community.

Dame Barbara has now written 617 books, the greatest number by a British author, passing the 564 books written by John Creasey.

AWARDS

1945   Received Certificate of Merit, Eastern Command, for being Welfare Officer to 5,000 troops in Bedfordshire.

1953   Made a Commander of the Order of St. John of Jerusalem. Invested by H.R.H. The Duke of Gloucester at Buckingham Palace.

1972   Invested as Dame of Grace of the Order of St. John in London by The Lord Prior, Lord Cacia.

1981   Received "Achiever of the Year" from the National Home Furnishing Association in Colorado Springs, U.S.A., for her designs for wallpaper and fabrics.

1984   Received Bishop Wright Air Industry Award at Kennedy Airport, for inventing the aeroplane-towed Glider.

1988   Received from Monsieur Chirac, The Prime Minister, The Gold Medal of the City of Paris, at the Hotel de la Ville, Paris, for selling 25 million books and giving a lot of employment.

1991   Invested as Dame of the Order of The British Empire, by H.M. The Queen at Buckingham Palace for her contribution to Literature.